AN HEIRESS FOR ALL SEASONS

Also by Sophie Jordan

AN HEIRESS FOR ALL SEASONS

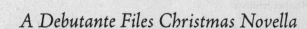

A Debutante Files Christmas Novella

SOPHIE JORDAN

AVONIMPULSE
An Imprint of HarperCollinsPublishers

Excerpt from *A Good Debutante's Guide to Ruin* copyright © 2014 by Sharie Kohler.

Excerpt from *Various States of Undress: Virginia* copyright © 2014 by Laura Simcox.

Excerpt from *The Governess Club: Louisa* copyright © 2014 by Heather Johnson.

Excerpt from *Good Guys Wear Black* copyright © 2014 by Lizbeth Selvig.

Excerpt from *Sinful Rewards 1* copyright © 2014 by Cynthia Sax.

Excerpt from *Covering Kendall* copyright © 2014 by Julie Revell Benjamin.

EPub Edition NOVEMBER 2014 ISBN: 9780062363633

Print Edition ISBN: 9780062363640

JV 10 9 8 7 6 5 4

For everyone who loves the holidays as much as I do . . .

...nar ...ent.

CHAPTER ONE

"**G**ood heavens. Violet, sit up straighter, we're almost there. These aren't ordinary people, you know. Try to look as though we belong."

Violet stopped short of rolling her eyes at her mother and pulled back her shoulders. She resisted the urge to peek out the carriage curtains. Mama was already peering through them and she refused to add her face beside her mother's, gawking like a child and advertising the fact that they did not, in fact, belong here.

Nor would they ever.

"Mama, you're letting a draft inside." She buried her hands deeper inside the winter muff in her lap and shivered. The heated bricks had cooled hours ago and she was eager for the warmth of a fire once they stopped.

"Oh, heavens!" Mama exclaimed. "It's a castle! Look, would you! Just think, Violet, this could all be yours if you play your cards right."

Violet squeezed her hands together until her knuckles ached inside her muff, refusing to take a look. What did she care about some grim, stuffy old house? Contrary to what her mother hoped—or thought—it would *not* be hers. A fact she did not give voice to. Not unless she wanted to send her mother into histrionics.

Adelaide Howard was determined that her only child marry a British nobleman. Born to an English merchant who immigrated to America over forty years ago, it was her most fervent wish.

"We're here!" Mama cried unnecessarily as the carriage jerked to a stop. "Now remember the manners they taught you at Miss Worthington's Academy. We didn't send you to that school so you could marry some no-account."

And by no-account, she meant John Weston, Papa's man of affairs. Violet had developed a tendre for him. She might have even encouraged him into asking permission to court her. Oh, very well, she had encouraged him, but only after he made his admiration for her known.

Mama had declared the match inappropriate, but that had not deterred Violet. Papa had come to rely on Mr. Weston on almost all matters and credited much of the continued success of Howard Iron Works to the man. She had been certain he would give his blessing. Except Papa, who most usually gave her anything she wanted, had refused. Mama, in turn, had reacted by booking them on board the first ship to England from New York City. To find a proper husband for Violet.

Sighing, she descended the carriage. Where she promptly gasped at the sight before her.

It was, indeed, a castle.

There was nothing grim or stuffy about it, either. The

Earl of Merlton's house was constructed of white brick and stood four stories high, stretching wide against the snow-draped countryside. It was everything light and airy and bright.

"Mrs. Howard, welcome, welcome!"

Lady Peregrine, the Dowager Countess of Merlton, descended the stone steps, extending her hands in warm greeting to Violet's mother as though they were old friends and not in fact acquaintances of a mere week.

Mama took her hands and bobbed an awkward curtsy that looked dangerously close to bringing Lady Peregrine down. "My lady, so kind of you to have us for the holiday."

"But of course! So far from home, I could not have you spending Christmas in a hotel. You shall spend Christmas here with us as our most honored guests." Lady Peregrine turned her bright eyes on Violet. "So nice to see you again, Miss Howard. How lovely you look in that fetching green."

"And you, too, my lady. Thank you for your gracious invitation."

There was the slightest pause as she assessed Violet, sizing her up, no doubt wondering if she would suit her son.

For that was why Violet was here, make no mistake. Although she had not met the earl when in Town, she knew Mama and Lady Peregrine had discussed him, and his readiness for a bride, at length.

According to Mama, this visit to Merlton Hall would end in a match between Violet and the earl.

"Come, let us relax with some refreshments in the drawing room."

The instant the lady turned her back Violet pressed her

lips into a mutinous line, vowing that this visit would be no more than that. A *visit* and not preliminary negotiations for the marriage that her mother predicted.

A short time later, they were joined in the drawing room by Aurelia, the earl's younger sister. At twenty years of age, she was unwed. Mama, who had done her research, informed Violet this was partly due to the earl's strained finances and that he could not provide a healthy enough dowry for his sister, and partly because she was a reputed termagant.

Violet and Aurelia eyed each other as they sipped tea and munched on iced biscuits. In truth, little was required from either of them as Lady Peregrine and Mama filled the conversation with very few breaks.

It was in one of these brief gaps in conversation that Aurelia finally spoke. "Tell me, Miss Howard, did you always know that you wanted to be a countess?"

Violet blinked. Mama gasped.

Lady Peregrine set her teacup down with a decided clack. "Aurelia!" she said in affronted tones.

"What, Mama?" She blinked innocently. "I'm merely curious if this has been a lifelong ambition of Miss Howard or merely something recent."

Violet squared her shoulders. "I confess it has never been a particularly important mission of mine, no."

"Indeed? Then how do you come to be in England, on the marriage mart, touted as one of the wealthiest heiresses of the Season?"

"Oh, Aurelia," Lady Peregrine collapsed back on the settee. "Must you say these things?"

Mama still sat there, unspeaking, her mouth agape.

"How does anything come to be?" Violet fluttered a hand in the air philosophically. "A good many things happen without planning or consent. I wager no one consulted you before dubbing you a termagant."

Silence descended on the room. Only the clock on the marbled mantle could be heard issuing its barest ticks. Mama's eyes were enormous in her face. That wide-eyed stare darted toward the door as though anticipating they would soon be booted through it.

Then, all at once, Aurelia arched her neck and laughed. "Oh, she would be a brilliant match for Will."

Lady Peregrine released a sigh and nodded. "I thought as much."

Mama grinned like a madwoman. "Indeed! You think so? Truly?"

"Oh, indeed." Aurelia nodded, her dark chestnut curls bouncing.

Violet sipped from her cup, muttering in a low breath, "Is everyone in this room stark raving mad with the exception of myself?"

Apparently her words did not go completely unheard. Aurelia only laughed harder. "Oh, I cannot wait for Will to meet you. Remember to be yourself."

Could I be anyone else?

Shaking her head, she resisted arguing that it would not matter. They would not be a *brilliant* match. She would not live in England. She would not marry some stuffy nobleman

who thought he was better than everyone else simply because
he was born with a title. She was going back to America. Back
to her Mr. Weston.

The rest of the day passed in a blur. They were shown to
their rooms and permitted to rest before dinner. Violet allowed her maid, Josie, to dress her in a gown Mama selected.
An elaborate deep gold confection that Mama swore made
her hair appear more blond than brown. She stared at herself in the mirror, not seeing that it made much difference.
Everything about Violet was just in between. Hair in between brown and blond. Eyes not quite green or brown. Just a
muddy hazel. Not quite tall nor short. Neither beautiful nor
ugly. Just in between.

Before venturing down to dinner, Violet stood before the
double doors of her bedchamber and admired the landscape.
The moon was bright tonight and seemed to reflect light off
the pristine white landscape. She had a perfect view of the
stables and itched to go down and examine the horseflesh.
Lady Peregrine mentioned they possessed a vast stable. Perhaps in the morning, she could beg a tour.

Another sigh escaped her lips. The house really was lovely.
As was Lady Peregrine. Even Aurelia had turned out to be
quite friendly. It would not be so bad a place to spend the
holiday, she decided. She merely had to keep the earl at arm's
distance and in no way encourage him. Hopefully, he would
not be so desperate for her dowry that he proposed on the
first night. That would make for an awkward visit. She could
visualize him so well in her mind. Like so many noblemen

she had met upon arriving in England. Pasty-white and soft all over. Palms that perspired when they danced and breath that reeked of garlic. She winced. Perhaps this would be an unbearable holiday after all.

To her relief, the earl did not make an appearance at dinner. Lady Peregrine could not hide her consternation. Even Aurelia looked annoyed.

"I was hoping to witness his reaction upon meeting you," Aurelia grumbled as they walked together down the corridor on the way to their bedchambers. "It would have been entertaining to say the least."

"I doubt it would have been very diverting. I'm really not that interesting."

Aurelia arched an eyebrow somewhat skeptically, stopping before Violet's door. "We shall see. Good night, Violet." She pressed a kiss to her cheek unexpectedly.

"Oh. Good night." She watched the girl move down the corridor and disappear inside her chamber before stepping inside her own room. Her maid soon arrived to help her undress for the night.

Alone in the vastness of her lavish chamber, she laced her fingers over her stomach and stared up into the dark. She wondered how many people over the centuries had slept in this room, in this very bed. Now she was here. An American whose ancestors could very well have been serfs on this grand estate.

And Mama expected her to marry this earl? Some pompous lordling who hadn't even seen fit to make an appearance yet. A wave of homesickness washed over. She missed the simple life she had left behind. Reading aloud after dinner to her Papa before the fire. And Mr. Weston with his kind, warm eyes. Always so kind. So respectful. She had to beg him for their first kiss, and even after that he still insisted on addressing her as Miss Howard. When Papa declined his suit and Mama announced their trip he had vowed to wait for her. To be faithful to her for all of his days even if that meant standing by as she married another man.

She sat up in the dark with an angry huff, flinging the counterpane back on the bed. She would not marry another man. She'd return home and eventually Papa and Mama would see just how perfect she and Mr. Weston were for each other. They'd relent. They had to.

Rising to her feet, she strode to the window again and stared out at the night, at the dark shape of the stable. A light glowed from within. Stable hands, no doubt.

Making up her mind, she fetched her boots and slipped them on. Finding her heaviest cloak, she put it on as well, burying herself in its ermine-trimmed folds. Pulling the hood over her unbound hair, she slipped from her chamber. The castle was as silent as a tomb. A doorman slept in a chair near the door, snoring softly, oblivious to her departure.

She sucked in a sharp breath when she stepped out into the night and burrowed deeper inside her cloak. She hurried, her feet eating up the ground as she rounded the house and drove a straight line for the stables.

She pushed open the creaking doors and stepped inside. The interior was marginally warmer. The smell of horse, sweet hay, and earthy oats immediately filled her nose. This felt like home to her. A light glowed from the far end of the stable. She could detect the faint sound of masculine voices. Deciding she needn't alert the stable hands of her presence, she strolled silently before the stalls, peering in at each horse, petting velvety noses and cooing softly.

She reached one stall, larger than the rest and immediately she understood why. Inside stood a monstrous beast of a horse. A black stallion with a white star on its forehead.

He stood back several paces, watching her warily, his liquid-dark eyes seeming to say, *I don't know you.*

Violet extended her hand, palm out, for him to sniff. "Come, my beautiful boy, come now. Let's see you."

The stallion walked a few steps closer, his hoofs hitting the ground almost reluctantly as he approached.

"There now, my beauty. I'm sorry I have no treat for you. Let me pet you, and next time I promise to bring you a tasty treat. Would you like that?"

Almost as though he understood her, he tossed his head, neighing, his glossy dark mane shaking on the air.

Then he did it. He pushed his velvety nose into her palm. His hot breath puffed against the cup of her hand in greeting. She grinned.

"What in the bloody hell do you think you're doing?"

Violet whirled around with a gasp, her hood sliding back from her head. A stable hand stood there glaring at her. He'd discarded his jacket and neck cloth. She gaped at the inappropriate sight of his lean physique on display. His shirt was open at the neck, exposing firm, touchable looking flesh. His trousers fit him like a second skin, concealing nothing of his narrow hips and muscular thighs. Dark boots hugged his calves almost to his knees. He exuded virility—the type of man who spent more time out of doors than indoors.

His face was equally pleasing. Square jaw. Sharp blade of a nose and piercing blue eyes. Eyes that looked her over now, taking in her tumbled hair and cloaked figure. Her hands dove for the edges of her cloak, making certain none of her nightgown peeked out. With consternation, she realized she still had not responded.

Remembering she was a guest here and not someone to be spoken to so rudely—by a stable hand, no less—she drew back her shoulders. "I was merely petting the horse."

His gaze flicked to the stallion just behind her.

"You're lucky he did not make a snack of you. I believe he has a fondness for Yanks."

She bristled, quite certain no servant or employee had ever talked to her in such a manner before. Certainly such ill manners were not tolerated in an earl's household. Perhaps he thought her a servant, too.

Lifting her chin, she disagreed. "He's quite friendly."

He crossed his arms over his chest, drawing her eyes there again—to that impossible broadness. "I know him. And he's not friendly."

She crossed her arms, mimicking his pose. "Well, I know horses. And he is. He likes me."

His eyes flashed, appearing darker in that moment, the blue as deep and stormy as the waters she had crossed to arrive in this country. "Who are you?"

"I'm a guest here." She motioned in the direction of the house. "My name is V—"

"Are you indeed?" His expression altered then, sliding

over her with something bordering belligerence. "No one mentioned that you were an American."

Before she could process that statement—or why he should be told of anything—she felt a hot puff of breath on her neck.

The insolent man released a shout and lunged. Hard hands grabbed her shoulders. She resisted, struggling and twisting until they both lost their balance.

Then they were falling. She registered this with a sick sense of dread. He grunted, turning slightly so that he took the brunt of the fall. They landed with her body sprawled over his.

Her nose was practically buried in his chest. *A pleasant smelling chest.* She inhaled leather and horseflesh and the warm saltiness of male skin.

He released a small moan of pain. She lifted her face to observe his grimace and felt a stab of worry. Absolutely misplaced considering this situation was his fault, but there it was nonetheless. "Are you hurt?"

"Crippled. But alive."

Scowling, she tried to clamber off him, but his hands shot up and seized her arms, holding fast.

"Unhand me! Serves you right if you are hurt. Why did you accost me?"

"Devil was about to take a chunk from that lovely neck of yours."

Lovely? He thought she was lovely? Or rather her neck was lovely? This bold specimen of a man in front of her, who looked as though he had stepped from the pages of a Radcliffe novel, thought that plain, in-between Violet was lovely?

She shook off the distracting thought. Virile stable hands like him did not look twice at females like her. No. Scholarly bookish types with kind eyes and soft smiles looked at her. Men such as Mr. Weston who saw beyond a woman's face and other physical attributes.

"I am certain you overreacted."

He snorted.

She arched, jerking away from him, but still he did not budge. Instead his hands tightened around her. She glared down at him, feeling utterly discombobulated. There was so *much* of him—all hard male and it was pressed against her in a way that was entirely inappropriate and did strange, fluttery things to her stomach. "Are you planning to let me up any time soon?"

His gaze crawled over her face. "Perhaps I'll stay like this forever. I rather like the feel of you on top of me."

She gasped at his shocking words.

He grinned then and that smile stole her breath and made all her intimate parts heat and loosen to the consistency of pudding. His teeth were blinding white and straight set against features that were young and strong and much too handsome. And there were his eyes. So bright a blue their brilliance was no less powerful in the dimness of the stables.

Was this how girls lost their virtue? She'd heard the stories and always thought them weak and addle-headed creatures. How did a sensible female of good family cast aside all sense and thought to propriety?

His voice rumbled out from his chest, vibrating against her own body, shooting sensation along every nerve, driving home the realization that she wore nothing beyond her cloak and night rail. No corset. No chemise. Her breasts rose on a deep inhale. They felt tight and aching. Her skin felt like it was suddenly stretched too thin over her bones. "You are not precisely what I expected."

His words sank in, penetrating through the fog swirling around her mind. Why would he expect anything from her? He did not know her.

His gaze traveled her face and she felt it like a touch—a caress. "I shall have to pay closer attention to my mother when she says she's found someone for me to wed."

Violet's gaze shot up from the mesmerizing movement of his lips to his eyes. "Your *mother?*"

He nodded. "Indeed. Lady Merlton."

"Are you . . ." she choked on halting words. *He couldn't be.* "You're the—"

"The Earl of Merlton," he finished, that smile back again, wrapping around the words as though he was supremely amused. As though she were some grand jest. He was the Earl of Merlton, and she was the heiress brought here to tempt him.

A jest indeed. It was laughable. Especially considering the way he looked. Temptation incarnate. She was not the sort of female to tempt a man like him. At least not without a dowry, and that's what her mother was relying upon.

"And you're the heiress I've been avoiding," he finished.

If the earth opened up to swallow her in that moment, she would have gladly surrendered to its depths.

CHAPTER TWO

T he heiress he'd been avoiding intrigued him.

This was his sole thought as he surveyed her. She was young. Pretty. Prettier than she realized. He recognized that at once. She did not possess an inch of self-awareness and that was a refreshing change. Most heiresses he had met floated around with inflated egos, confident that their positions and dowries would win them anything. The pretty ones were the most insufferable.

His fingers flexed against her arms. He itched to move his hands and grip the hips splayed above him, settle her to his liking against him. She was curvy. Her body soft and yielding. He appreciated the cushion of her breasts on his chest.

Perhaps his mother had finally found someone he could sincerely consider.

"Miss Howard, I presume."

If possible, her eyes widened even further. She nodded jerkily, all that unbound hair of hers tossing around her face and trailing down to his chest. He itched to touch the pale brown mass, gather it in his fist to test its texture.

"I don't recall your Christian name." Something with a V. Vera? Victoria? He really should remember. His mother had talked of her incessantly since she had extended the invitation for her to join them through the holidays. As though the constant barrage of her name and talk of her dowry would persuade him to propose.

It was apparent that no man had ever handled her thusly—or uttered suggestive words to her before. He knew that at once from her wide-eyed expression. Enough reason for him to peel her off him and stand, and yet he remained just so. She was a guest in his home. Worse than that. She had come here for the sole purpose of snaring him into marriage. He should be thrusting her from him and running in the other direction. And yet here he remained.

"My Christian name is Violet," she supplied, reminding him of a wild animal on the verge of biting or bolting. Her hazel eyes, so wide and gleaming green-gold, watched him without blinking. Her voice was husky, her accent soft and sultry.

"Violet," he pronounced, studying her—this strange creature so unlike the icy heiresses his mother had paraded before him in the hopes he would form a match and drag his family back from the brink of debt his father had left them in.

"I did not give you leave to use my Christian name." That chin of hers lifted. He knew she was trying for haughty, but she missed the mark. He knew haughty. He'd been surrounded by haughty all his life. There was something genuine about her. A female without airs or pretension. A girl who would sneak into the stables on a cold winter night wearing naught but a cloak and nightgown.

It was clear she hadn't known his identity . . . which made her reaction to him all the more interesting. Her face burned every shade of red. He was no green lad unable to recognize his effect on her. He felt her response to him.

Her body trembled against him. After her initial struggling, her curves sank pliantly into him. His body stirred, aroused.

"True. You did not give me leave," he finally answered. "Addressing you by your Christian name does imply a close acquaintance, but is that not why you are here? To make my close acquaintance?"

Her eyebrows knitted tightly. "I'm here because my mother insisted. She didn't want to spend Christmas at a hotel and—"

"She brought you here to win an earl," he finished, cutting straight to the matter.

Her mouth shut with a snap, her lips twisting obstinately, as though she refused to admit this glaring truth.

"Come. It's no secret that's why you are here."

"What my mother wants and I want do not necessarily match, my lord."

"Indeed? That would be a first." He studied her sharply, intrigued. A well-bred girl who did not bow to the whims of her Mama? What a novelty.

She frowned at him, distrust keen in her hazel eyes. "What do you mean?"

"A debutante that does not follow the instructions of her mama . . . an heiress with a decided lack of social ambitions."

"Rest assured, *this* heiress is not on the hunt for a title."

He stared at her in silence, wondering if this was some

manner of game. Was she toying with him? Pretending she had no wish to be a countess merely to pique his interest? Because it was working.

This girl . . . a brash American, no less, had sparked something in him. She was different from the rest.

Different good.

"Will!"

He looked up as Max strode from the back where they'd been playing a hand of cards with the stable lads. She took advantage of the distraction and jabbed him in the chest with her elbow.

"Oof," he grunted as she scrambled off him before he could stop her.

He rose to his feet, rubbing at his stomach, watching as she fled the long length of the stable lane without a glance back, her dark cloak whirling after her, revealing pale flashes of her nightgown at her ankles.

Max stopped beside him. "Who is that?"

He stared after her as she slipped from the double doors and out into the cold night, resolution stealing over him. He resisted the impulse to go after her. *Let her run. For now.*

Turning, he faced his friend. "That, Max, is my bride."

Max's eyes widened. "You jest."

He glanced to where she disappeared. "She is the first chit my mother waved beneath my nose that has inspired even a flicker of interest. So yes, I am quite serious. I'll have her."

"That's hardly reason—"

"I've dragged my feet long enough. I need to wed an heiress." His mother had been telling him so for years. He could deny it no longer. He alone was privy to his account ledgers.

And while he still held hopes the investments he made would eventually yield, something needed to be done now. "For the estate and my tenants. For mother and my sister . . . Aurelia needs a proper dowry now."

Max clasped his shoulder. "Will, you need only say the word. I can help—"

He flinched. The offer was made in all generosity, but it still stung his pride. Just as it stung when his cousin, Dec, had made the same offer to help him well over a year ago. He'd taken Dec's advice on a few promising business ventures, but there he drew the line.

He shook his head, cutting Max off. "It's my responsibility. My family and my people. It's time I do my duty, and Miss Violet Howard will do nicely."

The following morning, the Duke and Duchess of Banbury arrived. They were already at breakfast in the dining room when Violet finally emerged from her chamber. She'd slept abysmally after her encounter with the earl the night before. Upon entering the dining room, a single swift glance reassured her that he was not present. She released a relieved breath. She supposed she would have to come face-to-face with him eventually. Unless she convinced her mother to leave. To disregard that they had been invited to spend the holidays with an earl and instead take shelter in their hotel. She winced, imagining her mother's reaction to the suggestion. Not likely.

Introductions were made in short order. The earl's cousin, the Duke of Banbury, sat at the head of the table, his wife directly at his side. They were both young and attractive and seemed overly fond of touching one another. Nothing unseemly. His hand brushing her arm, her shoulder. Her hand atop of his on the table.

There was something in the angle of the duke's jaw that brought to mind his cousin and made Violet flush warmly. Or perhaps there was no real resemblance . . . merely an arrogance inherent to British noblemen.

Aurelia sat beside the duchess and it soon became apparent that they were close friends. Violet's mother talked more than usual—and louder—even for her. Clearly she was nervous to find herself in such prestigious company and felt the need to over-compensate with jarring and inane chatter.

Violet sank down in the chair beside Lady Peregrine, smiling numbly.

"Did you sleep well, my dear?"

She nodded and was on the verge of responding when the doors opened and two men walked in the room.

The air expelled from her lungs in a rush. It was him. Only not half-dressed. Thankfully. He was attired properly, all in black with a deep blue cravat at his throat. His hair gleamed wetly, swept back from his forehead as if he had just bathed. Even clothed, she still reacted at the sight of him. Her stomach pitched and rioted as if a thousand butterflies suddenly took up residence there.

"William, how good of you to finally put in an appearance and join us." Lady Peregrine's eyes danced with glee.

The earl rounded the table and pressed a kiss to his mother's cheek. His steely blue eyes found hers over his mother's head. "I decided I have been remiss in not properly socializing with our guests."

"That's very good of you to recognize that, my dear," she sniffed.

Ha! Remiss, indeed! He merely wanted to witness her embarrassment after yesterday.

Lady Peregrine turned her attention to her son's companion. "Maximus, so good of you to join us for the holiday, too."

He bowed over her hand. "I would not have missed it, my lady."

Lady Peregrine motioned to the two gentlemen, her gaze flitting from Violet to her mother. "Ladies, may I present my son, Lord Merlton. I told you he was not a ghost. Indeed he does exist. See for yourself. And this is Viscount Camden, our dear friend."

Mama babbled some greeting that ran on far too long. Violet could look nowhere other than his face. Those eyes which fixed so steadily on her. As though they were the only two people in the room.

She wrenched her gaze away and focused on the plate of food a servant had placed before her, hardly able to focus on the kippers and eggs.

A shadow fell over her and she forced her gaze back up, startled to find him so very near.

What was he doing staring at her thusly?

"Miss Howard." He reached for her hand where it rested limply beside her plate. "A pleasure to meet you."

Blood rushed to her face as he brought her hand to his mouth for a brief kiss.

She snatched her hand back the moment he released it and

tucked it under the table on her lap. Such gallantry. Did he toy with her? Lord Camden made no such move toward her. He merely watched, grinning in the same manner as everyone else. Well, except for the duke. He looked rather stunned, his lips pressed into a firm line. Like he did not know what possessed his cousin to lavish such attention on her.

Merlton seated himself across the table from her. She looked anywhere and everywhere but at him for the remainder of breakfast, listening mutely as Lady Peregrine discussed the Christmas festivities she had planned.

She imagined she felt the weight of his stare on more than one occasion, but dared not confirm her suspicion. Actually, it took a great deal of concentration to not look his way.

So much concentration, in fact, that she missed the thread of conversation entirely. She did not snap her attention from her plate until she heard her name repeated.

"Violet shall love to, won't you, Violet? Violet?"

She blinked, zeroing in on Mama's earnest face, nodding even though she was clueless as to what she was agreeing to.

"Splendid," Lady Peregrine clapped her hands. "Then we shall all meet back here before luncheon. May the best couple win."

Win? Couple?

Violet looked around then as everyone pushed back from the table with decided enthusiasm. Aurelia arched an eyebrow at her in bemusement. She leaned sideways to whisper, "You were woolgathering, weren't you? You haven't a clue what you just agreed to."

After a moment's hesitation, Violet nodded. "Yes," she whispered back. "What's happening?"

"You just agreed to partner with my brother on a quest for holly to decorate the house. Whoever gathers the most holly wins."

Blood roared to her ears. A quest for holly that would put her in proximity with the earl again? Alone? "Oh, no, no, I cannot . . ."

Everyone was already pushing back from the table and departing the room.

"Don't look so miserable. I'm stuck partnering with Camden, the scoundrel. I'll likely do all the work myself while he sneaks off to tumble a maid." At Violet's gasp, Aurelia blinked mildly. "Oh, did I say that out loud?" She shrugged. "Just count yourself fortunate you're paired with my brother. He knows every inch of this estate. He'll lead you to all the best holly and you'll be back here sipping chocolate while I'm still out there all by myself, finding nary a sprig."

"Are you coming, Aurelia?" Lord Camden hovered near the threshold, his boot tapping the floor impatiently, looking about as excited at the prospect of a morning in Aurelia's company as she was to be spending time with him.

Violet looked rather desperately at her mother as she departed the room arm in arm with Lady Peregrine, her face beaming, clearly thrilled that Violet had won a morning in the earl's company.

The room cleared out and they were alone. Again.

Not really alone. Everyone was within earshot. Just beyond the dining room doors. Their voices and laughter floated on the air.

"Shall we?" he offered her his arm. She fought the impulse to rush from the room. It was one morning. It meant nothing. If anything, a morning spent in her company would make it clear to him just how disinclined she was to the notion of marriage. She would make him understand that this was all her mother's idea—that she was not here with ambitions of becoming the Earl of Merlton's bride.

With a stiff nod, she placed her hand on his arm and allowed him to lead her from the room.

CHAPTER THREE

He pulled the sled over the snow-packed ground, looking over his shoulder to where Miss Howard—Violet—walked several strides behind. At first he thought he was walking too quickly, but he had slowed his pace enough for her to catch up with him. No. Every time he slowed down, so did she. She quite clearly did not want to walk beside him.

Turning, he stopped to face her. "Are you enjoying yourself, Miss Howard?"

She stopped and eyed him warily. Several feet separated them. Snow fell softly over them, lightly dusting their clothes. "Quite so." She nodded at the wintry landscape. "It's beautiful here. You must love it."

"I do. This place has been in my family for generations."

She nodded slowly, her expression serene, thoughtful as her eyes skimmed the countryside. In the distance, down the slope at the base of the hill, Merlton Hall nestled, stretched out like a sleeping beast.

He gestured widely. "My blood is in this land. In the people, the tenants here whose roots go as far back as my own." Hopefully his investments would bear fruit, but just in case, he must do right by his family and tenants.

"It must be nice to have roots like that. Papa built our house five years ago. It's a huge, ostentatious monstrosity just outside the city. Without heart. Mama wanted it to look like a castle. Versailles, I think she told the builder." Her lips twisted in a self-deprecating manner. "How can one replicate Versailles?"

"That would be a challenge," he agreed.

She released a breathy laugh. "Imagine living in such a place." Her gaze lifted to his. "The reason I'm here at all is because my mother is still reaching for something she hasn't found in America. She thinks she can find it here. Through me."

A mother living vicariously through her daughter. It wouldn't be the first time. But what did the daughter want?

Motioning to the sled, she asked in brusque tones, "Have we not gathered enough holly?"

"It's a contest. I intend to win." He looked her over as he uttered this, a slow grin curving his lips, and he realized he was only partially talking about this holly gathering expedition.

Her nose and cheeks were pink from the cold. Cloaked head to toe, her hands buried in a thick ermine muff, the rest of her face was a pale smudge. Pale brown wisps floated untidily around her cheeks. Wide eyes stared out at him, reminding him of a forest in spring, all greens and golds and browns. She looked young. Fresh and vibrant.

And she could be his.

The thought whispered over his flesh, leaving a trail of

goose bumps. She could be his and help him save his family from debt. Suddenly, the future looked bright indeed.

"What?" she asked, a telling tremor in her voice. "What are you looking at?" She slipped her hand from her muff and brushed at her face self-consciously with slim fingers.

"I'm looking at you, Miss Howard."

She dropped her hand back into the protection of her muff, but not before he noted the quiver of her fingers.

Her lips worked for a moment before arriving at the single word: "Why?"

"I enjoy it." *I enjoy you.*

"You enjoy looking at me?" She sniffed, her gaze darting nervously over the expanse of white around them before looking back at him. "I am so extraordinary then?" The utterance fell softly, with such skepticism. As though she doubted her own worth. Which was remarkable. She was attractive. Wealthy beyond reason. She had every nobleman in England sniffing about her skirts and she did not appear to especially hold herself in value.

Yes, he thought but held silent. She was extraordinary. She wouldn't believe him if he said that aloud. He could see that at once in the stiff set to her shoulders. She didn't consider herself different. Or special. And that only made her all the more appealing.

He tore his gaze off her, afraid he was revealing too much, too soon. Last week, he'd shared his bed with not one but two different women and had been plotting to woo a particular opera singer he'd seen perform. Now he had suddenly made up his mind to marry. That opera singer was forgotten. The only woman he could even focus on was the one before him now.

His cousin had uttered something months ago, following his marriage to Rosalie. *When you find the right woman, spending the rest of your life with her will be a simple decision because it's the only decision. The only thing that matters.*

He mentally shook himself for such fanciful thoughts. Of course Dec was in love with Rosalie, and Will had only just met Violet Howard. He didn't love her. He didn't know if he ever would. He didn't know whether the kind of love Dec and Rosalie shared was even possible for him.

But choosing to marry Violet Howard? That had been easy. Just as Dec had said. She was the right woman.

She was the first debutante to hold his interest and not make him want to walk a hard line in the opposite direction. That accounted for something. It accounted for a great deal.

He nodded in the direction of a thicket ahead. "I know one more place where the holly grows dense. You're not growing weary, are you, Miss Howard? Is such activity too rigorous for you? We could rest."

That chin of hers lifted as he suspected it would. "I am not in the least wearied. I am accustomed to walking. At home, it is a frequent habit of mine."

His mouth quirked. "Better, I take it, than staying within the walls of your miniature Versailles?"

"Very astute, Lord Merlton . . . and true." She strode past him, lifting her skirts and stepping high over the snow-laden ground.

He fell in behind her, pulling the sled. It slid with a soft swoosh over the snow. Still grinning, he cast her an assessing look. "Are you not enjoying my company?"

She slid him a look, her hazel eyes bright with suspicion.

"Deny and I appear rude. Agree and I'm the coquette. How shall I answer that?"

"Honestly," he returned.

Stopping, she crossed her arms. "Honestly? Very well. I'm here at the behest of my mother. I have no intention of marrying anyone while I'm in England. I apologize for coming here under false pretenses, but there you have it."

He dropped his grip on the sled's handle and settled his hands on his hips. "You came all this way . . . allowed everyone believe you were hunting for a titled husband and it's all a *lie?*"

She lifted one shoulder. "If you knew my mother, you would lie, too. It's easier to go along with her scheming and feign agreement than fight her."

He scratched his jaw and lifted his face to the cold air. "There's only one flaw with this . . . plan of yours."

She blinked, several snowflakes piling in her lashes. "And what would that be?"

"What happens when a man that fits your mother's criteria proposes marriage?"

She visibly relaxed, the line of her shoulders easing. "Oh, well, that hasn't happened."

"Yet."

"I beg your pardon?"

"That hasn't happened yet."

She paused before replying, clearly processing this. He could see the wheels in that clever mind of hers turning. "I'm sure I can avoid such an occurrence."

"Are you now?" He stepped closer. "So sure?"

"Indeed, I haven't encouraged any man's suit enough for him to make an offer."

He nodded sagely. "True. You're not the most inviting of females. Declaring yourself opposed to marriage to prospective suitors isn't the best method to gaining offers."

"Quite."

"And somehow, despite that, I find you . . . palatable."

Her smile faltered. "Palatable?"

"If I must marry an heiress, it might as well be one I find palatable. Your avowal not to marry a nobleman makes you precisely the sort of heiress I want for a wife."

She inhaled, the red tip of her nose quivering. "That makes no sense. What are you saying?"

He closed the last bit of distance between them. Her head dropped back to gaze up at him. Her eyebrows winged up over her hazel eyes. Those eyebrows were the same pale brown of her hair, on the thick side but well-shaped. Expressive. Especially paired with those unusual eyes. She could hide nothing. She was an open book, guileless, every emotion there for all to see. He could watch her face and all its sifting expressions for hours. A rather nauseatingly romantic notion, but there it was.

"You understand my meaning well enough. I'm saying that you will do, Miss Howard."

Her eyes flashed, the gold shards sparking in the green depths. "I will *do*? Is that your idea of a proper proposal?"

"Shall I go down on bended knee in the snow then? I did not think such a gesture necessary. You hardly strike me as a romantic, but very well. Far be it from me to withhold ritual—"

"No!" She grabbed hold of his arm and tugged, stopping him from lowering to the ground before her. "You're mad! You cannot mean it."

"I assure you proposals are not something men issue without complete sincerity."

She gaped at him, still clinging to his arm. "Then no! My answer is no." Her grip loosened and she took a hasty step back as if suddenly aware of their proximity. Her throat worked as she swallowed. When she spoke again, her voice was more even, controlled. "Even if I was interested, your proposal would hardly entice me." Her lip curled in distaste.

"Ah, wounded your vanity, did I? Shall I use other methods to coax you into acceptance?" His gaze skimmed her, wishing they were some place where they had no need of cloaks . . . where he could better reacquaint himself with the curves he had felt last night.

He reached for her and she jerked back, losing her footing and falling in a tumble of skirts into the snow. "Stay away from me."

He reached down to help her up, but she scrambled back, snow flurrying around her. "Don't touch me."

Crossing his arms over his chest, he frowned down at her. "Come, now. I'm not so unappealing, am I? There's something between us. You felt it last night. . . ."

"No." She shook her head, the hood of her cloak falling back, her expression a little wild, desperate. "No. I . . . there is someone else."

He froze, staring at her face—into eyes that could hide nothing. Tell no lies. Which meant she was telling the truth. There was someone else. Some other man who held her affections. Intense and sudden hostility toward this stranger surged through him.

"Who?" he demanded, a heaviness sinking in his gut.

"Someone back home."

"And why did you not marry him?"

She clambered back to her feet. "He's my father's man of affairs. Papa would not give his blessing."

"He's ineligible then. You should move on—"

"I don't care if he's deemed ineligible!" Her words flew like arrows at him, hot indignation coloring her cheeks. "I only care that he wants me. That he loves me." She points at her chest. "Me."

His hands opened and closed at his sides. "Are you so certain of that? He's in your father's employ. Perhaps he sees you as a way to further himself?"

She shook her head. "Not everyone is like you, searching for an advantage, cold calculation guiding every—"

He reached for her. This time his fingers closed around her arm through her cloak. "I've had plenty of opportunities to wed an heiress. You're the first one I've asked. I assure you cold calculation does not guide me in this."

She snorted, leaning back as he tugged her closer. "I'm supposed to believe you're overcome with sudden love for me? I'm not that gullible."

He winced. "I said nothing of love, but there are other considerations."

"None worth me forgetting my Mr. Weston. Or myself for that matter and jumping into marriage with you—"

"This other man," he cut in, his voice biting. "Weston. Where is he now?"

She blinked. "I told you my parents refused—"

"So while he's in New York, you're over here letting your mother parade you on the marriage mart. You might want to question his devotion to you."

"Mr. Weston knows I won't marry someone else. I told him I wouldn't."

"And still." He tsked. "He let you go. What a weak and paltry love is his."

The color rode higher in her face. "You know nothing of him!"

"Only that he does not deserve your loyalty."

"What was he supposed to do? We didn't have my father's blessing. We both agreed to wait for Papa to change his mind."

"I wouldn't have waited." He brought his face closer, lowering his head until his mouth hovered a mere inch from hers. "I would not have let you cross an ocean. You would already be mine. You would already sleep in my bed. You would wake with my mouth on yours every morning."

She exhaled and he tasted her sweet breath. Her hazel eyes flared wide, more gold than green right then and he knew he was scandalizing her, but better she knew who he was. What he wanted.

How it would be between them.

"Of course," she sneered, shaking herself slightly. "Because I'm an heiress. You couldn't risk letting me slip away." She cocked her head. "We wouldn't even be having this conversation if I was just a simple girl without a dowry. Would we?"

He stared at her, unable to deny that. The only reason she was here was because he needed to wed an heiress and his mother had invited her. They would have never even met otherwise. He made a point to stay away from the ballrooms of the *ton*.

"I thought so," she answered for him. Satisfied, she wrenched free and began slogging through snow in the direction of the house.

"Where are you going?"

"I think we've gathered enough holly." She paused and turned to face him. "I know you like to win, but sometimes in life ... you simply lose." That said, she turned and began descending the slope toward the house.

He watched her go, certain she wasn't talking about the holly, and equally certain that if they were playing a game, he would win.

CHAPTER FOUR

He wanted to marry her.

The notion should not have left her so shaken, but it did. As did his words about Mr. Weston. She had never doubted Mr. Weston. Or herself. It wasn't fair that a few words from one arrogant nobleman should suddenly make her question her feelings for Mr. Weston ... or Mr. Weston's ability to permit her to cross an ocean without him. Even if it was a ruse and she was pretending to go along with her mother's matrimonial scheming, he had not appeared too bothered at the prospect of her entertaining the suits of other gentlemen. He'd accepted the situation with unflappable ease. Too much ease? She frowned, considering the possibility that perhaps he did not care for her as much as she believed.

Shaking her head, she pushed such thoughts away and loosened her lips lest anyone see her scowling. Sipping from her spoon, she avoided the earl's gaze throughout the midday meal even though she felt his blue eyes assessing her across the table.

She attempted to listen to the Duchess of Banbury describe the months she had spent in Scotland following her marriage to Banbury. They had eloped and then remained there, returning to Town only a few months ago.

Violet felt certain there was more to the story of their hasty marriage, but none they were sharing.

Lady Peregrine pursed her lips. "Your wedding should have been the event of the year. I'm still most vexed with you. I wasn't even present!"

"I was," Lord Camden volunteered. "It was quite lovely. The bride was glowing." Smiling, he saluted the duchess with a lift of his cup.

"I'm certain Rosalie was beautiful," Aurelia chimed in, "Although the reminder that you were present while my mother and I were not is of no comfort." Her eyes gleamed more topaz than brown right then as she glared at the viscount.

His smile slipped and he glared right back at her.

The duchess shook her head. "Be nice, you two. Remember, 'tis the season of goodwill and charity."

The viscount nodded once at Aurelia. "Tell that to her."

"Oh, I'm perfectly charitable . . . to those deserving." Grinning, she lifted her glass at the viscount in mock salute.

"Aurelia, be kind. The viscount is a guest—"

"He's not a guest, Mama. He's always underfoot. As common as that old stool in the drawing room in desperate need of refurbishing from the constant abuse of Will's boots. . . ."

Color stained the viscount's cheeks and his lips compressed as though he were fighting back a response.

"Aurelia." Will's voice rang with quiet command. "Enough."

With a lift of her chin, she closed her mouth and focused her attention on her plate.

Violet studied the earl, intrigued how one word from him held such command. She doubted there were many people that Aurelia obeyed, but it was clear the girl respected her brother.

As though he felt her stare, his gaze snapped to her. She started with a small jerk to find herself the subject of that intense blue gaze. Even though he only stared at her face, she felt stripped bare sitting there with everyone else surrounding them. As though he could really see her. And perhaps he did.

Even after only just meeting her, he perhaps knew her better than anyone else did in this country. For he knew the one thing she had not told another soul since leaving home. That she would marry no one here. That she would live a spinster rather than marry a man who wanted her for only the fortune she brought him. She would rather be alone than spend her days with such a man. He knew that and still he looked at her as though he would gobble her up, clearly indifferent to the audience around them. She fidgeted on the seat.

Aurelia leaned close to whisper in indiscreet tones, "I believe someone is fond of you. You have achieved the impossible."

Clearly, she meant others to hear. Titters broke out along the table. Mama and Lady Peregrine beamed, looking back and forth between Violet and Lord Merlton.

"You're being fanciful," Violet murmured.

"My sister has been described as many things, but never fanciful, Miss Howard. She's a bit of a pragmatist."

Heat scalded her cheeks. It was virtually a declaration. He was implying that his sister was right and he fancied her.

Violet bit back the response burning on her tongue: *You are fond of my dowry.*

His lips lifted in a crooked, irresistible grin.

Oh, why, of all places, had they come here? Why must she be tempted by *him*? Why not a dim-witted man with putrid breath and missing teeth? The idea that she could have him, his smiles, his attention, was enticing. Only it wouldn't be real. She would be giving up on herself if she surrendered to the illusion of that. That life would be a lie, and even on the best of days she would always know that.

To be fair, it wasn't that she didn't trust him as much as she didn't trust herself. Yes, he was handsome. Beautiful, even. But she wasn't so weak to let that guide her. It was his intensity. His confidence. When he looked at her . . . and said the outrageous things he said, she felt alive. Every nerve in her body tingled and broke loose from slumber.

She had not even realized she had been living and walking around half-awake until now. Until him. He made her feel breathless and anxious and thrilled and nauseated all at once.

"Perhaps you don't know your sister as well as you think you do," she countered, ignoring her mother's small sound of displeasure beside her. "There's a bit of the fanciful inside everyone."

He clung to his smile, but his eyes changed . . . hardened with something akin to determination.

This time, she didn't look away. She let him drink his fill of her and read the resolve in her own expression.

Violet spent the next three days avoiding the earl. No easy feat with matchmaking mamas involved.

She knew she couldn't avoid him entirely for the remainder of her stay, but she could make certain they were never alone again. She glued herself to Aurelia's side whenever possible, never straying far as they hunted for a Christmas tree or arranged holly and decorated beribboned boughs throughout the house.

The man was trouble. He made her doubt herself and all her carefully laid plans. He made her doubt . . . *everything*. With a satisfied nod at her reflection in the dressing table mirror, she exited her bedchamber to join the others for dinner downstairs, smoothing a hand over her gold skirts. Ever since Papa told her that it made her eyes glow like a lion's, it had been a favorite. Even Mr. Weston complimented her when he had seen her wear it.

A sudden thought slid through her mind, jarring her as effectively as a window slamming shut. *Would the earl like it?* As quickly as the aggravating thought arrived, she banished it with a sharp intake of breath. His preferences did not matter.

"You're avoiding me."

She gave a small yelp at the deep voice so close to her ear. Whirling around, she faced the glowering earl. "You frightened me."

He stepped closer in the corridor, the breadth of his chest pushing at her bodice. Instantly, her breasts tightened. She stepped back hastily, furious with her body's treacherous reaction to him.

Her body had never felt like this before . . . as though it was its own entity, apart from her. Not even when Mr. Weston kissed her had she felt so . . . had she *felt*.

A breath shuddered past her lips. A situation that was drastically unfair. She and the earl had not even kissed—nor would they ever—and yet he made her entire body sit up and take notice.

She backed up until she collided with the wall, her hand drifting to her hammering pulse at her throat.

"And how is it that I frighten you?" He was close enough for her to marvel at the darker ring of cobalt rimming the silvery blue of his eyes.

"Because you startled me, my lord. That is what I meant to say. Startle. Not frighten."

He shook his head, a lock of dark brown hair falling over his brow. "No. That's not it. *I* frighten you. Today . . . yesterday," he growled. "You see me and run in the opposite direction."

True. She had kept her distance when they scoured the countryside for the perfect tree to grace the grand ballroom for Lady Peregrine's upcoming Christmas ball. It had taken the better part of two days to find the right tree to satisfy Lady Peregrine. Thankfully, the countess finally spied the massive fir because it had begun to snow in earnest then. It was still snowing. So much so that Lady Peregrine worried if the weather would hamper travel for the guests who had still yet to arrive.

In the shelter of the group and tromping about the countryside, it had not been too difficult to avoid him. She had stayed close to Aurelia and the Duchess of Banbury—that is when the duke wasn't whisking his wife away to sneak a kiss behind some shrubbery. Such displays were quite unusual to witness. Violet's parents hardly spent any time together. She had thought that was the standard for most married couples, but the duke and duchess were making her reconsider her view of marriage and all that it could be. Perhaps it could be something wonderful. Perhaps her eyes could shine and she could appear in a state of constant exhilaration like the Duchess of Banbury? She tried to envision a future like that with mild-mannered Mr. Weston.

She tried to imagine him grabbing her around the waist and pulling her behind a tree. She tried and failed.

The earl continued, his handsome expression perplexed, "Have you any idea how difficult it is to woo you when you won't stand within five feet of me?"

She fought back a smile. "Have *you* any idea how awkward it is for me to make certain I am never within five feet of you? You're wasting your time. I cannot marry you."

"You can," he countered.

"Very well." She lifted one shoulder. "I won't."

He flattened one hand on the wall beside her head. She followed the long line of his arm. He'd discarded his jacket and she could make out the cut and definition of his bicep and shoulder against the fine lawn of his shirt. Gulping, she looked back at his face, only that was not much better. Her stomach flip-flopped at his intense expression. "I can change your mind. Let me court you. . . ."

She looked rather helplessly around him, trying to decide how best to step past him without touching him. Because touching him would be a bad thing. She knew this deeply, innately. Experience had told her as much, as well. She had touched him in the stable, after all, when she had been splayed over him. No part of her hadn't touched him then.

That memory was still fresh enough to keep her tossing and turning at night.

"No," she uttered. The single word dropped like a stone between them.

He angled his head, studying her as though she was some species he had never seen before, and she realized she might be the first female to ever refuse him.

"I can be creative," he murmured softly, his mouth hovering an inch from hers and sending her belly into wild flutters. "I can continue to corner you, stealing moments whenever I can."

Panic shot down her spine as his gaze flicked from her mouth to her eyes. She could not survive a week of that!

"That's courting? Hardly romantic, my lord," she scoffed. "Sounds more like stalking . . . badgering. . . ."

"Call me Will."

"No." It wouldn't be proper and it would confuse her into thinking they were more than they were.

"I'll call you Violet."

She shook her head. "Don't do that."

He continued like he hadn't heard her. "Violet," he spoke her name as though he tasted it. The heat in her face intensified. He smiled then and she felt true danger beneath the seductive curve of his lips. "This Weston fellow? Did he kiss you?"

She blinked. "What an impertinent question!"

"I take that as a yes."

Heat scored her cheeks. Yes, he had kissed her. She supposed it could be called that. A quick press of his mouth to hers. She had thought it might last longer . . . that his dry and rather chapped lips might move over hers. True, she really didn't know how it was done. It was her first and only kiss, but she had thought it might be . . . well, it might be . . . *more*.

Immediately guilt flayed her for such a thought. John was a gentleman. Her thoughts were undeserving of him.

"That's all right." The earl nodded once, his eyes at once intense and feral on her face. "It doesn't matter. Because when we finally do kiss, you'll forget all about him. I'll kiss you properly. Or rather, improperly. I'll show you how it should be between a man and a woman and then you'll forget what's-his-name. You'll only think of me . . . and my mouth. . . ."

Heat washed over her. "You a-arrogant . . ." she stammered, searching for a word foul enough.

"It's true. We would be good together. Can't you feel it?" He cocked his head and motioned between them. "It's not like this with everyone."

"Oh, here we go again. I'm something extraordinary . . . you and I share something special." She laughed with a roll of her eyes. "What rot."

He lifted his hand so suddenly that she flinched. He waved his fingers slightly as though to prove he was harmless. She silently berated herself for being so skittish.

Those fingers landed on a loose lock of her hair along the side of her face. He rubbed the tendrils between his fingers as though testing them out. "Like wheat in morning sun." Her chest tightened at the almost reverent utterance. "So soft. I'd wager all of you is this soft."

Her breath caught, mesmerized even though she knew he was doing this on purpose—trying to addle her thoughts and seduce her with his words. He was an expert seducer, she had no doubt. A man like him . . . with his looks and position, he probably need say nothing at all for the ladies to titter and throw themselves in his path.

He leaned closer, his body encroaching until his breath fanned her ear. "Would you like me to show you how it can be? What your Weston can never give you?"

The tightness in her chest became unbearable. So tight she could scarcely breathe. She shook her head fiercely even as she gazed at his well-carved lips, imagining them on her, the pressure, the taste.

Blast him! He was a sorcerer. She would not be one of those debutantes to let him woo her with pretty words. She knew what he wanted and it wasn't *her*. Not truly her. This was merely a game to him, and she a conquest. "No. I would not."

And just like that he stepped back.

She blinked, surprised at his abrupt departure, almost falling forward after him. She was certain he had meant to kiss her.

"I will wait until you are ready."

She squared her shoulders, telling herself she was relieved. He would not kiss her. Good. That was very, very good. She was *not* disappointed. "Then you shall have a long wait."

"I'm a patient man. You will say the words. If not in speech, then in deed. I'll await your express invitation." He motioned between them. "Then this will happen. You. Me. And we shall wed."

The cheek of the man.

"It will never happen. I leave in a week," she reminded him. She could hold out that long and resist him.

His mouth curled in that insufferably melting way again. "A lot can happen in a week." The words were flung down boldly, confidently, but something lurked in the silvery blue of his eyes. Concern that perhaps a week would not be enough?

She stepped around him, confident that she could resist him now that he had just promised not to touch her. She merely had to endure the sight of him, ignore his persuasive words . . . and this attraction she felt whenever near him.

And yet knowing he would not touch her . . . that the curiosity he had piqued in her would never be satisfied left her feeling a little hollow inside.

No more than how hollow you will feel married to a man who wanted you only for your fortune.

With that thought bouncing through her mind, she hastened ahead of him down to dinner.

CHAPTER FIVE

For the next few days, he plagued her precisely in the manner he had promised. He was around every corner with a flirtatious smile or a clever compliment. One night she even found a bouquet of flowers on her pillow. She had no idea where he had found flowers in the midst of winter, but she knew he had. She knew they were from him.

His behavior had not gone unnoticed. Their mothers watched on, beaming at him with approval. And then their gazes changed when they looked at her. The approval altering to consternation for it was clear she went out of her way to discourage him.

"What's the matter with you, you daft girl?" Her mother barreled into her chamber one evening. "The earl *likes* you and you're treating him like a leper!"

Violet shrugged, meeting her maid's sympathetic gaze in the mirror. "Unfortunately, I don't like him."

Her mother stared for a long moment before groaning and pacing a hard line behind her where she sat at the dressing table. "Violet, you cannot expect to snare a better catch than Merlton. He's young and handsome—"

"And titled," she inserted forcefully. "Don't forget that. That's all you care about, is it not? Not whether he wants to marry me for me. Simply that you get an earl for a son-in-law."

Her mother stopped in her tracks to gawk at her. "Leave us," she announced to the maid, her gaze never leaving Violet.

Josie slipped from the room.

Her mother wasted no time. "You think John Weston wants you for you?" Her lip curled in a sneer.

Violet flinched. "Y-Yes. He doesn't care one whit for—"

"He cares for nothing as much as advancing himself, rest assured of that. You think he is so much better than Merlton? Then you're a fool!"

She bit her lip, considering her mother's words. Mr. Weston had been in her father's employ a long time. Before her father's business had even launched into the great success it was today. In that time, he had always been kind to her and shown interest. She had assumed his affection for her had been genuine, but could she be mistaken? Was he like every other fortune hunter?

Her mother pressed on. "In any case, it might be too late. Another heiress just arrived with her family. Apparently Lady Peregrine didn't place all her hopes on you. They were delayed due to the snow, but even now she is downstairs simpering and working toward winning over your earl."

Violet stifled another flinch. "He's not *my* earl. And the actions of a female I don't even know hardly concern me. She's welcome to Merlton."

Her mother shook her head, her eyes suddenly a little sad. "Tread carefully, Violet. It is now, in these very moments, that you shall decide the course of your life." With that parting comment, her mother left the room.

The silence of the empty bedchamber swallowed her as she sat alone at the dressing table, her mother's words reverberating inside her.

Her name was Felicity Little and she was the only child to one of Britain's largest and most profitable sugar importers. Violet and Miss Little were perhaps of similar wealth—but there the similarity ended. She was tiny with curling, golden hair and enormous china-blue eyes. Her laughter was infectious. Tinkling and occurring with steady frequency, she laughed gaily and talked with confidence and wit. Even Aurelia seemed to like her. Everyone nodded, smiling as she regaled them with a humorous tale of her recent visit to the Spain and how she had ridden a goat up a mountain pass.

Violet wanted to stab the girl's perfect eyes out.

A totally unprecedented sentiment. Such acrimony wasn't like her and it shamed her. She didn't want the earl. She had told him so in no mincing terms. She had confessed as much to her mother. So why did she sit so miserably as the earl hung on Miss Little's every word? Poking at a bit of potato on her plate, she watched the two of them from across the table with narrowed eyes, her fear quickly dissipating that Merlton would catch her staring. No chance of that. His eyes were only on Miss Little.

Contrary man! He was exactly as she thought. A money-grubbing fortune hunter. She had proven too elusive so he had moved on to the next available heiress. She should be relieved, not angry, to be right in her estimation of him.

Upon finishing dinner, they rose to move to the drawing room. Apparently, Miss Little was an accomplished vocalist. She had agreed to perform Christmas carols for them.

Violet's eyes suddenly burned as the earl offered Miss Little his arm and led her from the dining room.

"Miss Howard, are you coming?" Viscount Camden gently touched her arm, his eyes kind as they studied her.

Blinking once, she forced a smile up at him and nodded. "Yes, thank you."

"Shall we?" He offered her his arm. Accepting it, she fixed the smile on her face and allowed him to lead her forward.

Miss Howard—*Violet*—excused herself early from the drawing room as Miss Little finished singing "Good King Wenceslas," complaining of an aching head.

Will watched her intently as she moved across the room, studying her pale face and listening as she made her excuses to both their mothers. Aching head, his arse. She was fleeing him. Again. As she had been doing from the very beginning. He released a pent-up breath.

He tracked her as she slipped from the room, silent as a wraith as Miss Little launched into another carol.

"What are you doing?"

At the mild question, he turned to face Max beside him. "What do you mean?"

"You've been chasing after Miss Howard since you first clapped eyes on her." He nodded to where Violet had departed. "I thought for certain you were on the verge of declaring yourself, and now you're suddenly panting after this little

Nightingale here." He nodded toward Miss Little and then chuckled. "Little Nightingale."

Rolling his eyes at the jest, Will shrugged, not caring to discuss matters of the heart in the midst of his family's drawing room. He hadn't given up on Violet. On the contrary, he had simply decided to give her some space for a day or two, and let her consider the loss of his attention. He was wagering that she would miss said attention—that she would miss *him*—and come to her senses. And perhaps paying attention to Miss Little would make her realize that all the sooner.

"You're no longer interested in Miss Howard, is that it?" Max rubbed his chin thoughtfully, apparently unwilling to drop the subject. "Good to know. This house party is getting a little tedious. I confess she appeals to me ... and there is a good deal of mistletoe about. I wouldn't mind some diversion. A man could lose himself in her eyes. And that voice. ..."

"Max," he growled, but his friend continued as though he hadn't heard him.

"You know me. I like a female with some curves. Something to hang on to as you plow—"

The rest of Max's words were lost. Will's fist shot out to connect with Max's runaway mouth. The two crashed from their chairs to the floor. The ladies cried out, jumping to their feet. Dec and Mr. Little quickly wedged themselves between him and Max.

Will strained to break free, swiping his arm for one more blow.

"Will, what's gotten into you, man?" Dec shook him, and it was only then that he realized Max wasn't struggling for another go at him.

No. Max was grinning, his white teeth a blinding flash in his face as he tentatively touched his bottom lip where a cut bled profusely. "Just as I thought," he announced.

Will stared, gaping at his friend, realizing that Max had been toying with him, knowing how he would react.

Dec stepped back, watching him carefully should he need to restrain him again. Max marched forward and clapped Will on the shoulder, whispering for his ears alone. "Whatever game you're playing, you're going to lose. You're going to lose *her*."

Something heavy sank in his chest at Max's words. Nodding and realizing he'd made a colossal mistake that just might cost him the only woman he had ever wanted beyond the span of one night, he faced everyone. "My apologies. Just a quarrel among friends."

"William?" His mother asked, her eyes clouded with worry.

"We're well now, Mother," he assured her even though the last thing he felt was *well*.

Was it possible to feel this way for a woman in so short a span of time? So desperate and heartsick at the thought of losing her.

It could happen, he realized. She could walk out of his life as easily as she had entered it. He swallowed against the sudden thickness in his throat. She could return to America and her Mr. Weston without a backward glance.

Max clapped him on the shoulder, addressing his mother, "Nothing to fear, my lady. We're still the best of friends."

She nodded, a wobbly smile gracing her lips.

"If you'll excuse me." Will motioned to his mussed clothing as though it was something he cared about and must attend to.

Striding from the room, he took the stairs two at a time, intent on one goal. One female. As long as she was still here, there was a chance—and that's all he needed to fight.

O nce inside her bedchamber, Violet turned in a small circling, feeling suddenly as if she were suffocating. She told herself that she would be gone from this place in a few more days. And yet a few days seemed much too far away. She needed space. Distance. Air to breathe. Tired of being cooped up, she marched toward her armoire and began riffling for her warmest clothes. Garbed appropriately for the elements, she slipped from the room and took the servants' stairs out of the house. She tromped through the snow to the stables.

The stable lad tried to stop her, but she ignored him as she saddled her own mount, a gentle mare named Daisy. The only thing she could see was Merlton's face in her mind, watching raptly as Miss Little shared her goat-riding anecdote. If Violet had told such a vapid story would he listen with even a fraction of such interest? Blast the man! Why must she care one way or another?

She was tempted to take Devil for no other reason than irking the earl—assuming he ever peeled himself from Miss Little's side to notice she had left the room—but she knew that might be pushing the stable lad beyond his limit.

"I won't go far," she assured him. "And it's not yet full dark."

He gestured helplessly. "Miss, the snow. . . ."

"It has stopped."

"Aye, but it could begin again. I feel it in my bones. My bones always know." He bobbed his head insistently. "And you could lose your way out there in all that. The landmarks are—"

"I've spent a good amount of time over the last week walking the estate. I am quite familiar with the lay of the land." She had to leave. She had to get away. She didn't care if it was bitter cold. She couldn't stand another minute in that house whilst Merlton courted another heiress. Would he use the same words? Would he tell her just how *good* they could be together? *Blast!* Fire scraped the back of her neck and crept over her ears.

"Allow me to saddle up my mount and accompany you."

Using the block, she mounted Daisy with sure movements, relishing the feel of a horse beneath her. She missed this. This was familiar. Safe. An earl with silvery blue eyes and a devil's tongue was not. She looked down at the stable lad. "That's not necessary. I'm an accomplished rider. I will be back shortly." She just needed a little air. Space and distance. Another moment beneath that roof walls while the earl courted his new heiress and she might go mad.

He twisted his cap in his hands, still looking uncertain and she smiled down at him with the same smile she bestowed on Papa when she wanted to win her way. It rarely failed her.

He relented, although still looking unhappy. "Please don't be long, Miss."

"I promise. I'll be back soon." Nodding, she lifted her scarf high against her throat and dug in her heels.

She rode out from the stables, determined that a brisk ride

would help her forget. At least for a little while she could forget herself. And the earl who filled too much of her thoughts.

"What do you mean she left?" Will waved a hand toward the partially open doors through which he had just passed. It had begun to snow again, and a screen of white fell at a sharp angle outside the stables.

After searching the house for Violet and finding no sign of her, he had decided to check the stables, recalling the first night he met her. He knew how much she enjoyed the horses. She was bold enough to brave the cold and visit Devil again. It would be like her not to shy away from the bitter weather. Or a stallion that bites. The girl was fearless. Or at least she put up a brave front. It's what drew him to her—her flashing eyes and bold words. And made him want to wring her neck.

"I tried to tell her. . . ."

Will did not stand around to listen further. He made short work of mounting Devil, a dark fury brewing inside him. The reckless fool. What did she think she was doing?

"Inform His Grace and Lord Camden I've gone after Miss Howard," he tossed over his shoulder. "Not a word to my mother. She will only worry. Banbury will do what he deems best."

He guided Devil from his stall. Tom hastened to pull the door wider for him.

"Careful, my lord. Visibility is right poor in this weather."

Precisely why Violet had no business riding out into it. He nodded curtly. He wasn't worried for himself. Blinded by snow or not, he could find his way home.

"Let no one set out after me, Tom. I know this country-side better than anyone else."

Tom nodded.

He only knew one thing. He would not return empty handed. He'd find Violet or die trying.

CHAPTER SIX

Contrary to what she promised the stable lad, Violet wasn't finding her way back home any time soon. She accepted this grim fact not half an hour after she departed the stables. It had started to snow again, and by the time she turned back, it was already too late. The sky opened up and unleashed itself.

Everything was doused in white, the snow falling in an opaque curtain, obscuring her vision.

She forced herself to breathe in the bitter, frozen-wet wind, pushing down the panic that threatened to smother her as she scanned the horizon.

Everything looked the same. The snow-draped landscape. The fir trees shrouded in white. The path was gone, eaten up in swirls of wind and writhing snow flurries.

Burrowing into her thick garments, she told herself that she would be well. That this situation was not as desperate as her mind screamed.

Trusting Daisy to have a better sense of where shelter could be, she loosened her grip on the reins and gave the mare its lead, telling herself to have faith in the animal's instincts since hers had so clearly failed her.

Trust in Daisy . . . in God's plan. She blinked, trying to shake off the clumps of white clinging to her lashes as she squinted ahead.

Keep moving. Don't stop.

As long as she kept moving, Daisy would find the house, they would reach civilization eventually. She convinced herself of this, filling her mind with encouraging words, telling herself she had not sentenced herself to death. She would not die. She still had so much to live for. So much to experience.

The earl's face—*Will*—flashed across her mind and for the first time, she did not push the image away. She let him fill her thoughts. She let the rush of his memory give her strength and fill her with a longing ache.

Out of the swirl of wind and snow, a dark blur appeared on the landscape, coming into sharper focus the closer she advanced. Her heart jumped alive, thumping hard against her ribcage. It wasn't Merlton Hall, but it was shelter.

It was life.

Will scoured the countryside, his shouts gobbled up in the wind and snow, but there was no sight of Violet. He fed the weak hope that she had returned home. That even now she was warming herself by the fire in his drawing room with his mother and sister and Rosalie fussing over her. Still, he pushed on, unwilling to put his faith in that slim shred of hope. There was more countryside he had yet to cover. Until he did, until he'd satisfied himself that he had looked everywhere, he would not return.

The familiar crofter's cottage loomed ahead. The Jacobsons had vacated the cottage last spring, hoping to find work in the city. Another failure, he had deemed, on his part to properly care for all his tenants.

It occurred to him that if he had happened upon the cottage, Violet might have done so, too. She might have taken shelter within. It was the sensible thing to do. Riding out on the brink of a snowstorm hadn't been sensible at all, but he wouldn't put it past her to have a moment of good sense. Perhaps her need for self-preservation had kicked in at last.

He quickly led Devil to the barn to investigate, falling back against the wall in relief and scrubbing both hands over his face at finding the familiar mare there, unsaddled in one of the stalls, munching serenely on coarse, long-forgotten hay.

He dismounted and quickly tended to Devil, securing the stallion in another stall while the wind howled outside, knocking at the structure's walls.

Pulling the collar of his coat high around his ears again, he jogged across the yard, sinking to the middle of his boots. He closed a hand around the latch and pushed the thick door in, entering the cottage, his heart rising up in his throat in that moment, the irrational, remote fears still there, clinging to his clammy-cold skin.

What if he stepped inside an empty room? What if she was still out there? *Still lost to him?*

Wind and snow swirled inside with him, the door clanging against the interior wall.

She was there. Lips blue-tinged, teeth chattering loudly enough for him to hear where he stood . . . but alive.

He took a long blink, relief rushing over him. His eyes opened, watching her push up with one hand from where she had been kneeling, stoking the fire to life, her eyes wide and luminous in her pale face. The elegant arrangement of hair his mother had complimented her upon at dinner was a thing of the past. Only the remnants of it remained, tumbling in disarray down her shoulders. He preferred it this way. The firelight licked over the thick mass, gilding the damp waves.

He reached for the latch and closed the door, shutting out the moan of wind, reducing it to a mere whispering drone in the world beyond their shelter. The fire was already at work, creating a toasty haven from the winter raging just outside.

He rubbed a hand at the back of his neck, feeling its tremble and knowing it was a release of his anxiety. Another emotion took its place, snaking over him, eating its way into muscle and bone, heating his blood to a steady simmer.

Anxiety faded, and fury replaced it.

"M-My lord? How did you find me?" Her gaze jumped from him, flicking to the single bed in the modest dwelling, a reminder that she had likely never stood near a bed and a man simultaneously. Flags of color marred her cheeks and she suddenly became fascinated with the toes of her boots.

"Will," he said, the growl of his voice unrecognizable to his ears. He couldn't remember ever feeling this angry with another human being. Not even upon his father's death, when he learned the extent of damage his sire had wrought upon the family's finances, had he felt this level of fury.

"I told you to call me Will." Of all the things he could

have said, this was the only thing that stuck, the only words he could manage. It struck him as ridiculous ... annoying and insulting that she would still address him by his title. Especially considering they would marry. More than ever now he was determined that this would happen. Someone had to keep her from killing herself. Clearly, she needed him. Now it was time to make her realize that.

He glanced around the cottage. It would be their accommodation for the night. Perhaps longer, depending on the storm. She must realize that this would require they marry.

He faced her again. Those wide, unblinking eyes of hers looked him over. He glanced down, following her gaze. The dark of his cloak was hidden beneath the powder of white covering him. Even now he could feel the snow seeping into his pores from his soaked garments. She could be no better. She'd hung her cloak on a peg near the door, but he could see her dress hung heavy with damp upon her shivering body. The fabric molded perfectly to her breasts and his gut stirred with an emotion other than fury.

He removed his cloak, unbuttoning it and flinging it from his shoulders. He hung it on the peg near the door and then started on the buttons of his waistcoat, his movements brisk and efficient.

"W-What are you doing?"

"Removing my wet garments. You need to do the same." He draped his waistcoat over the back of a chair and then pulled his shirt over his head in one motion.

Her eyes widened, and she held out a hand, palm face out. "Please! Stop!"

"Don't be foolish. Undress."

Her chin shot up, the familiar fire back in her eyes. "I will not!"

He inhaled swiftly and advanced two steps before forcing himself to stop, curling and uncurling his hands at his sides. "You realize you could have died out there tonight. And for what?"

"It wasn't that bad when I left—"

"Are you seriously trying to suggest that you used good judgment? That you *weren't* foolish?" He waved at her. "You will undress yourself, Violet . . . or I will do it for you."

Equal parts terror and excitement raced down her spine as Will squared off in front of her, his chest bare, smooth skin stretched tight over firm-looking muscles that beckoned her questing fingers.

She'd never been alone with a near-naked man *and* in such proximity to a bed before. It was scandalous, but she was certain the circumstances would forgive the breach in impropriety. As long as nothing improper occurred between them. As long as they maintained a respectable distance—*and she remained clothed at all times.*

She moistened her lips. "You wouldn't dare."

He sank down into a chair and tugged off his boots. "Have you noticed that we're both wet and freezing with naught but that fire and these walls to keep us from freezing to death?" His boots thunked to the floor. He looked back at her. "And each other. So, yes. I do dare."

She shook her head. "It's highly improper—"

"We're past propriety." He rose and advanced on her with long strides.

She yelped and ran. Not that there was anywhere to go. At the wall, she stopped and turned, her back digging into the rough-hewn wood.

He halted in front of her, looking mildly bored. His bare chest lifted on a deep breath. "You're being foolish."

"Oh, foolish again, am I?" She flung the words out, still stinging over his earlier accusation.

"Yes," he countered.

"I was doing just fine on my own. I found shelter. Started a fire. You didn't need to come after me. I don't know why you did! Shouldn't you be proposing to Miss Little by now?"

He propped his hands on his waist. "I don't usually propose to one female once I have already decided to marry another."

She inhaled, fighting back the small thrill his words gave her. For whatever reason he was fixated on her, he still only wanted her for her dowry. It was tempting to forget that. She couldn't permit herself to do so. "You cannot mean—"

"You. I mean you. I haven't changed my mind."

"I haven't said yes." *She wouldn't say yes.* "In fact, I've said no."

He folded his arms across his chest. Her eyes roamed the cut of his biceps before snapping back to fasten on his face.

"You think you have much choice now?"

His knowing expression infuriated her. She stamped one foot. "You planned this! You followed me and—"

"Oh, I *planned* that you would be daft enough to ride out tonight? I *planned* this snowstorm? I *planned* for you to find this cottage?"

She shook her head, too angry to admit that she was being

unreasonable. "I won't be forced into marrying anyone. So you can find yourself another heiress! Your Miss Little should do well enough. She appears fond of you."

One corner of his mouth kicked up. "You're fond of me."

Oh, the maddening man! "Keep telling yourself that and you're going to lose out on not one but two heiresses. Your precious Miss Little is going to slip between your fingers if you don't—"

"You sound jealous." His smile turned smug. "You don't need to be."

"Jealous?" She laughed, but something shaky jumped inside her chest and her face burned hotter. "That's absurd."

His hand shot out to circle the back of her neck. Her laughter died at the sensation of his fingers on her neck, pulling her hard to him, trapping her between him and the wall.

All levity fled his expression. His deep voice roughened as he uttered, "I couldn't give a bloody damn about Miss Little."

She shook her head, but his hand tightened on her neck, stopping the movement. His eyes drilled into her, relentless blue. "It's time we had an understanding, you and I."

His head descended and the treacherous thought drifted through her head. *Finally.*

She didn't have time to examine that sentiment as his mouth claimed hers in a kiss that was nothing like the one she'd experienced before. There was nothing tentative or gentle or *safe* about it.

For a moment, she could hardly move, too stunned at the pressure of his mouth on hers, at his chest crushing hers.

He lifted up slightly to growl at her, his eyes flashing, "Open your mouth to me."

She wasn't sure if she obeyed because he commanded her to or because the mere boldness of his words made her gasp. Either way, her lips parted and his mouth was back on hers again.

He brought one hand to hold her face, his thumb beneath her chin, tipping her mouth higher for him.

He kissed her bottom lip, then her top lip, briefly pulling it between his teeth. She moaned. His mouth slanted over hers, kissing her deeper. His tongue slid within. He licked along the inside of her mouth. Her hands gripped his shoulders, clinging to him as though she feared he would stop—that he would take this new and exciting thing away from her. His tongue touched hers. Stroked it once. Twice.

"Move your tongue against mine," he breathed into her mouth.

With a partial nod, she touched her tongue to his. He made a low sound of approval. She felt it vibrate from his chest to hers as she mimicked his kiss, stroking his tongue back.

His arms wrapped around her waist and lifted her off her feet, mashing her breasts into his chest—breasts that felt aching and heavy in a way she didn't know was possible.

Then she was moving. His hard body walked her to the bed, his mouth never breaking from hers. He brought her down on the bed, never parting with her, coming over her.

He kissed her forever, holding her face with both of his hands like she was the most treasured thing in the world to him. Desire pumped thick through her blood. Her hands roamed his arms, his back, reveling in the firm flesh.

"You are wearing entirely too many clothes," he growled against her mouth.

She nodded and made an incoherent sound of approval as his fingers worked the buttons free down the front of her damp bodice. He yanked the jacket of her habit open and tugged it free of her arms with anxious movements. She lifted half up off the bed, eagerly accommodating him. He tossed it over his shoulder. It hit the floor with a smack, and he went to work on her stays. He paused once he had stripped her down to her chemise, sitting back and devouring her with his eyes.

Her chest lifted high on sawing breaths. His eyes were the color of a winter storm now, icy blue, the dark ring of cobalt almost black. His fierce expression absorbed her— first her face and then her bared shoulders, drifting down to the nearly translucent fabric of her chemise. He cupped her breast through the thin fabric and she moaned as his deft fingers stroked her, working so surely, so confidently. A sharp cry tore from her as he found her nipple and pinched it, rolling it between his fingers.

"P-Please," she choked.

"Please what? Say my name," he commanded.

"Will, please," she begged, without knowing what she was asking.

His mouth closed over hers again in a blistering kiss. He settled between the voluminous folds of her skirt and she growled, her legs fighting against the heavy fabric, hungry for the feel of him.

"Violet," he whispered into her mouth, and the hoarse sound of her name from him undid her. Something snapped then—a fine thread of control severed. Everything became frantic and feverish.

She dragged her palms down his back and gripped his

backside in a desperate move to pull him closer, to bring him against that aching part of her.

He cursed and lifted off her. Instantly she felt bereft, aching until she realized his intent was to remove the last of her garments. She responded to the swift pressure of his hands directing her to turn one way and then another as he stripped the last of her clothes off.

Then she was naked.

Not even Josie had seen her bared in such a way. So exposed and vulnerable. He sat back a moment to observe her, raking her with eyes that burned, scalding her everywhere they looked.

Propped up on her elbows, she was panting, gasping, and shaking on the bed. The urge to cover herself was there—but not nearly as strong as the urge to have him over her again—his mouth, his hands, all of him.

"W-Will?" she queried, bewildered at his utter stillness.

His gaze fastened on her face. "You're beautiful, Vi." His throat worked as he swallowed. "And you're mine."

He hopped off the bed in one swift move and divested himself of his trousers. She hardly had time to look her fill of him before he was back over her, his smooth, firm flesh surrounding and sliding against her.

She gasped at the sensation, the shock of a man *naked*. Against her. He slid down her body, his mouth everywhere, at her breasts, her stomach, her hips, then lower. *There*.

She clutched fistfuls of his hair, arching up off the bed with an astonished cry. "Will, what are you doing—"

He splayed a hand on her belly, pushing her back down on the bed, his lips moving against her. "Tasting you," he growled, his tongue working against her and doing delicious, impossible, *improper* things that left her writing on the bed. Her hands groped, searching for something to hang on to.

Then his fingers were there, too, stroking her, finding that secret, buried spot and rubbing it in circles, pinching it, squeezing until small, unrecognizable sounds erupted for some place deep within her.

He added his mouth again and sucked that tiny button between his lips, scraping it with his teeth until she came apart, until she shuddered and cried out as great ripples of sensation claimed her.

He came back over her then, his bigger body a hard, wonderful weight on hers even though he braced himself on his elbows on either side of her head. His expression was both tender and feral as he stared down at her, smoothing the hair back from her face.

He held her gaze as he settled between her thighs, nudging them wider.

Her stare fluttered down, scanning the tops of his broad shoulders.

"Look at me."

At the whispered command, her eyes snapped back to his stormy gaze.

"It's going to hurt for a moment."

She nodded, not fully comprehending his words, only lifting her hips instinctively as he she felt him pushing inside her.

She closed her eyes, her head falling to the side, throat arching as she felt him inch in, stretching and filling the aching core of her.

"Open your eyes. Look at me, Violet."

Opening her eyes, she was instantly snared in his intense blue stare. There was no part of her that didn't feel claimed and possessed by this man.

And he wanted that, she realized as his palms flattened with hers, pinning them above her head, their fingers lacing together. She didn't care. She wanted it, too. This. Him.

He drove deep, lodging himself inside her, breaching her maidenhead. The pain was fleeting. She was too awed by the sensation of him buried inside her, the pulse and pressure of him within her.

He held himself there, watching her face. She wiggled her hips, adjusting, experimenting, whimpering as the clenching throb flared to life at her core again. His breath hitched, and he pumped his hips, pulling out and entering her again.

The friction made her eyes flare wide. "Oh!"

"It just gets better," he promised against her mouth, increasing the tempo, driving into her faster, harder. She met his thrusts, crying out at every impact, straining against his hands.

His fingers tightened around hers, holding fast as his body moved over hers, stoking her to a frenzy. The pressure in her coiled and tightened until it released in a great burst. Colors sharpened. A shrill cry spilled loose from her throat as she arched against him.

He released her hands. Her arms remained limp at her sides as his hand slid along her thigh, bringing it up and around his hip, lifting her leg as he stroked inside of her several more times until he cried out and spent himself, shuddering his release.

"Violet," he gasped in her ear, rolling to the side and bringing her with him. Face-to-face, they panted, neither moving.

She opened her mouth several times to say something but fell silent. What did one say after sharing such intimacy? He watched her face, his eyes tracing her features as though committing to memory.

She sat up and reached for her clothes.

He stopped her with a hand on her arm. "No need for that. We won't be going anywhere until morning, and if you dress, I'll only be undressing you yet again before the night is done."

"Again?" She had not thought this the type of thing one did multiple times in a day, but then what did she know of the act? Her cousin, Marianne, confessed her husband only visited her in the dark and lifted her skirts to perform the necessary deed. They never saw each other naked.

Apparently Will was not like cousin Marianne's husband . . . nor would marriage to him be like the one Marianne had. Considering Marianne looked perpetually bored, this was not a bad thing,

With a start, she realized she was beginning to view marriage to Will as more than a possibility.

His mouth lifted in a half-smile. "Yes. Again." His hand held her face, long fingers spearing through her hair. "You and I are only getting started."

His mouth closed over hers again, and she let herself be swept away. It was so easy to surrender. Much easier than talking about the future and what precisely this would mean for the both of them.

CHAPTER SEVEN

A distant shout brought Will hard awake. He hopped from the bed, shivering as he left the warm bed and the warm, yielding female body nestled against him.

Scrubbing the heel of his hand against his bleary eyes, he moved to peer out the window. Dec and Max plowed through the snow with several stable lads behind them.

"Who is it?"

He turned at the soft voice. "Help has arrived."

She was a fetching sight, sleepy-eyed and tousled—a woman well and thoroughly bedded. Anyone would know at a glance. They'd slept very little, dozing into slumber just before dawn. He was responsible for that, unable to keep his hands off her.

He should have stopped after their first joining and given her untried body time to recover, but he had behaved like a randy youth. "Quickly, dress yourself. They'll be here any moment."

She darted from the bed like the hounds of hell chased her. "What shall they think?" she muttered, bright flags of red staining her cheeks.

"They'll think we took shelter amid a storm."

Her jaw clenched and he winced at the reddened skin there from the scrape of his bristly jaw. He'd have to be more careful with her delicate skin in the future.

She shook her head. "Mama must be scandalized—"

"I'm certain she will be relieved that you are not a frozen corpse lying out on the countryside. In addition to that, I'm certain she will be delighted with our marriage."

Violet froze, her hands at the buttons of her riding habit. He held her gaze, daring her to object even as a part of him was nervous that she would. Which was absurd. When had he ever been nervous over a woman?

She moistened her lips and his gut tightened at the small dart of her tongue along her lips. Lips slightly swollen from the previous night.

Bloody hell! He was insatiable. He couldn't understand it entirely. He'd known women. He and Dec and Max had burned a path through countless boudoirs in Town. He'd never feared rejection before. Why should he? There were plenty of willing women happy to share their beds with him. He'd never cared one way or another for one woman. Until now. Until her.

He only knew that he felt an overwhelming need to possess her, have her, keep her with him always. And he wanted her to feel the same way about him.

"I suppose," she murmured, the usual fire that drew him now banked in her eyes. "Marriage is the thing to do after last night."

He nodded, wondering why her voice rang so hollowly. "Quite so. After last night there is no escaping that fact."

She nodded. "Quite so," she echoed, removing her cloak from the peg beside the door and swinging it around her shoulders with smart, efficient movements. Cold. Mechanical. Not at all like the Violet he had come to know and crave with every fiber of his being.

"Very good. I'll speak with your mother as soon as we reach home." Nodding, he pulled the door open for her and motioned for her to precede him outside.

With a nod and bracing breath, she stepped out ahead of him into the cold.

The snowstorm abated enough for the last of the guests to arrive. They had been trapped just down the road at a nearby inn, but with the sun breaking through the skies, they forged ahead in their carriages.

With only two days before the Christmas ball, no less than forty people occupied Merlton Hall. The house was full of carols and delicious smells and parlor games. Even now, the sound of merriment could be heard from down the hall. If Violet wasn't so conflicted, she was certain she would be enjoying herself.

"So it's agreed then? We shall make the announcement the night of the ball?" Lady Peregrine fairly bounced where she sat on a wingback chair across from the crackling fireplace in the earl's office.

"Agreed." Will nodded, his voice solemn.

"I've always adored Christmas, but this is turning into the merriest Yuletide I can recollect! I shall have the housekeeper set aside the best champagne. There will be much to toast." The countess nodded, her turbaned head bobbing happily.

"Indeed, I shall send word at once for my husband. We agreed he would only make the voyage once Violet secured a groom. We didn't know how long it would take."

Violet winced, unable to meet Will's gaze at her mother's crass statement. *Secured a groom.* She made it sound as though she were procuring fish at market.

"Indeed, Mr. Howard must be here for the wedding and that shall give us plenty of time to plan properly. It must be at St. James."

Mama giggled and clapped, her face flushed with her excitement and Violet wanted to crawl into a hole.

Still fighting to keep her gaze off Will where he casually leaned against his desk, she rose to her feet, "If you'll excuse me. It's been a long day."

"Of course, my dear." Lady Peregrine nodded sympathetically. "We can discuss this later. We have plenty of time."

Nodding, she turned to leave. In doing so, her gaze caught Will's. He watched her with an intent expression, his eyes drilling into her. She commanded her limbs to move, to flee. Even as she departed, she could hear their mothers launching into a discussion of the wedding.

At least they were happy.

She, on the other hand, didn't know what she was feeling. Safe in her room, she allowed Josie to help her undress for the evening, her thoughts churning.

"Thank you, Josie. That will be all."

Her maid left and she approached the double doors to peer out the glass at the winter landscape. She supposed she should feel guilty. Perhaps even ashamed of herself. She was giving up on Mr. Weston after she had promised him that she would return to marry him. If she were honest with herself, there hadn't been anything of substance between them. The *idea* of him had intrigued her more than anything else. She recognized that now.

And yet she was still giving up on Mr. Weston to marry a fortune hunter.

Without guilt. Without shame. The moment he had kissed her in that cottage, she had known this would be the outcome. She had accepted that. Resigned herself to the fact that she would marry a man who only wanted her for her fortune. If not for Howard Iron Works, Will would not have asked for her hand. Somehow, even knowing this, she would learn to live with herself.

Sighing, she dropped her forehead to rest against the cold glass, staring into the snow and feeling suddenly weary.

"Going to bed early, aren't you? You're missing the festivities."

She whirled around with a gasp, everything in her coming instantly alert at the sight of him in her bedchamber. "Will! What are you doing in here?"

She had not even heard him enter the room. He approached slowly, his strides long, measured. Like a predator closing in on its prey. "You don't seem like you're enjoying yourself. And you've been avoiding me. Again. Did you think I would not notice?"

She belted her robe and shook her head, inching away from the French doors, deliberately keeping space between her and the bed. She sidled along the wall, palms skimming the surface. "I'm fine. Merely tired. You shouldn't be here, what if someone saw you enter my room? What if they see you leave?"

"No one did. No one will. And even if they did, our marriage is imminent." His eyes were intense again, drilling into her in that searching way. "Correct?" he pressed.

She blinked. He almost sounded uncertain. "Our mothers are planning the grand event even now, are they not?"

"But what of you? What are you planning? What do you want?"

"I-I," she faltered. She wanted to marry a man who loved her. She wanted to marry *him*. Unfortunately, the two did not seem inclusive. Shaking her head, she started past him. "Now you ask that? Isn't it enough that I'm marrying you? What more do you want from me?"

He seized her by the shoulders and pushed her back against the wall. "I want you to want this, but I'm getting the decided impression that you don't."

"I made it clear in the cottage what I wanted."

Something sparked in his gaze. Those flashing blue eyes slid over her. His hand moved to the tiny ribbon at the front of her nightgown. "This then?" he asked, lowering his mouth to her neck. His hot breath fanned against the shell of her ear as his hand dipped inside her nightgown to cup her breast. "You want this. I know it . . . I can tell by the way your eyes flare, your breath hitches."

"Y-Yes, no," she moaned, her head falling back on the wall as his thumb rolled over her nipple.

"If this is what you want, I can give you this."

It wasn't all she wanted. She wanted so much more. And yet it was a start.

His hand moved to the front of his trousers, freeing himself before coming back to her and hiking her nightgown up to her hips. He lifted her off her feet, wrapping her thighs around his waist and entering her in one slick thrust.

She cried out, fingers digging into his shoulders as he withdrew and surged deep inside her again, pushing her higher against the wall. She clung to him as he moved in and out of her, his hands cupping her bottom. It was swift and furious, each stroke pushing her closer and closer to a precipice.

She bit down on him through his jacket to muffle the little sounds escaping her.

"God, Vi, you're made for me."

She came apart in his arms, her cry lost in the hard press of his shoulder. As she drifted back down to earth she marveled at herself—at this creature she had become. Had she always been this? So wild and wanton? It only took a man like him to come along and expose her true self?

He plunged several more times until his own release took him. He shuddered against her, his hands clenching where he gripped her bottom. Their chests rose and fell against each other, their panting breaths mingling.

She lifted her head to find him waiting, watching her. After a moment of his heavy scrutiny, she patted his shoulder with a shaking hand. "Would you mind putting me down now?

He obliged, allowing her to slide down the length of him. He didn't move right away, which was probably a good thing. Her legs had the consistency of jam. Her hands fluttered between them, like birds unsure where to land. After such intimacy, it was silly that she should feel so hesitant about touching him. Even now she practically felt the hammer of his heart vibrating from his chest into hers.

"A female that does not fill the aftermath of lovemaking with chatter . . . you are a true anomaly. I would not mind knowing your thoughts."

His invitation to discourse could not be any more direct, but her thoughts were too troubling to share. She was disappointed for reasons she dared not share.

At her silence, he sighed and stepped back. Suddenly able to breathe again, she moved away from the wall. She smoothed her hands over her nightgown, attempting to regain her composure.

"You better go." She pressed her palms against her sides to quell their shaking. "Before you're discovered." *Before the world knows precisely how wanton and lacking all restraint she was.*

Tension feathered his jaw as he tucked himself back into his trousers with hard movements. Nothing in his demeanor revealed shame or regret over their tryst. "I'll go, but the time will come when we're married and you cannot hide from me. We will be bound to each other. We will share a bed. A life. You will have to share your thoughts . . . you will have to talk to me."

She bit back a caustic response. Why should he care what she thought . . . whether or not she hid herself from him? They'd be wed. He'd have her fortune. Why need he concern himself with her?

"Say something, damn it," he bit out. "Instead of looking at me with those big wounded eyes." There was something in his voice right then . . . something almost anguished, which made utterly no sense.

"What shall I say? You have me." She waved both arms. "You've won my fortune."

Angry color swept over his face. He motioned between the two of them with a sharp flick of his fingers, his blue eyes blazing. "Is that all you think this is between us? A mere business merger?"

"Don't insult me by insisting it's more. The only reason I was even invited here was because of my fortune."

"And the only reason you came was because of my title," he retorted.

"That was my mother's doing! You know I care nothing for your title!"

"What then do you care about?" he charged, taking a swift step toward her. "I can't believe you've agreed to marry me if you wish otherwise. Have you not come to care for me even a fraction? Have you no tender feelings for me at all?"

It was her turn to blush—she felt the heat creeping up her face. "That would be foolish. We just met." Her pulse hiccupped at the base of her throat. She looked him up and down, striving to be casual and unaffected—to reveal none of her panic at how close to the truth he struck. "It must be your other assets that won me over. That and finding myself stranded overnight with you."

He glowered at her, his lip curling over his perfectly straight teeth. "Indeed. Most convenient that bedding me is no chore."

She lifted her chin defiantly and sought to look unaffected. "It's some consolation." Only some. He needn't know that she cared for him with a desperation that frightened her. That what she felt for him was more than desire.

That she had fallen for him.

His wit, his confidence, the kindness in which he dealt with his mother and sister. All of it coupled with the butterflies that erupted in her belly at his very nearness. She supposed that was love. *Blast!* Of course, it was. For no other reason would she have surrendered so easily to his seduction. For no other reason would she cast aside her dignity and marry a man who wanted her for her fortune. All this she realized, but she held her tongue.

He moved toward the door, his hard strides biting into the carpet. She blinked back the sudden burn in her eyes.

At the door to her chamber, he paused and motioned between them. "I won't say this won't happen again. It will be a few months until the wedding and I'm not a patient man." His gaze raked her, and she did not mistake his meaning. He wanted her. He enjoyed her. But for how long?

How long until the desire he felt for her ebbed? How long after their marriage, her fortune secured in his coffers, until he ceased to want her?

She nodded, revealing none of her insecurities. Her heart was already bound to him. He did not realize it, but as long as he wanted her, she was his. He need only look at her, touch her, and she would surrender.

"Of course." She fixed a smile to her lips. "As you said. Bedding you is no chore."

His jaw clenched at the echo of his earlier comment. Without another word, he turned and left the chamber.

CHAPTER EIGHT

"Violet! Oh, Violet! Wake up!"

Violet jerked awake at her mother's ungentle hands.

"Mama?" She propped up on her elbows on the bed. Early morning sunlight streamed through the window. She frowned, thinking she was usually up at dawn. This was what came of tossing and turning through most of the night.

Her mother waved a piece of parchment in her face. "This came by special messenger just now."

Violet snatched at the missive. "What is it? Is something amiss? Did something happen to Papa?"

"Oh! Oh!" she huffed. "Something has happened!" She laughed shrilly, pacing beside the bed, her silk skirts swishing. "Something happened indeed!" Casting a look over her shoulder as though she feared someone could be listening, she dropped down on the bed beside Violet. "We're ruined! We've lost everything!" she hissed.

Violet blinked, the last shred of sleep-induced fog evaporating from her head. "What? How is that possible?"

"Oh, read! Read for yourself!" Mama motioned to the wrinkled parchment.

Her gaze lowered to scan the missive. She read the words without comprehending so she read them again. And again.

She lifted her stare to her mother's tear-ravaged face. "It's all gone?" she murmured numbly, her voice whisper-soft.

"John Weston," her mother sneered. "You thought him so charming and noble. You and your father both placed such trust in him. Well, he took it all and fled. A warrant has been issued for his arrest, for all the good that will do. He's probably halfway to the islands by now."

Violet's stomach sank. She pressed a hand there, convinced she would be sick. Mr. Weston embezzled Papa's fortune? As the implications of this sank in, full understanding dawned. He must have been doing it all along. Perhaps if she had married him, he would have stopped, satisfied that he had married her father's sole heir, but after she left for England to find a husband, he must have decided to abscond with his ill-gotten gains.

"Oh dear God! What shall I tell Lady Peregrine?" Mama's wild gaze darted to Violet, hopeful and beseeching. "Perhaps we can not mention anything and hurry the wedding along—"

"No," Violet pronounced, her voice flat and emotionless despite her inner tumult. "We won't resort to trickery or lies."

Her mother's shoulders slumped. "Very well. I suppose we can't do that." Her gaze scanned Violet's face. "You don't suppose Merlton would want to marry you anyway? Perhaps he's truly fond of you—"

"No," she said again, staring straight ahead into nothing, not even looking at her mother. "He's not fond of me." Not enough. She was the one who had gone and lost her heart. He hadn't. She was the one whose heart was dying a slow death inside her right now. "He was only after the dowry. His family needs it. He can't marry me now." She wouldn't demand it of him. No matter how utterly compromised she was, she wouldn't force his hand. He needed an heiress, and she was no longer that.

Mama nodded morosely, tears tracking swiftly down her cheeks. "I know. I know. 'Tis so hard to give up the dream, you know? And we have nothing now! Not a penny to our names. . . ."

"We shall make do." Violet patted her mother's shoulders as she gave way to tears once again. They would make do. Nothing could feel worse than this. Than the thick, suffocating press of knowledge that she would never feel his arms around her again. She would live the rest of her life without him.

"Who will have you now, Violet?" she wailed.

"Shh," she soothed. "All will be well." Now wasn't the time to tell her mother she would never marry. There would never be anyone for her. Not after Will. Instead, she said, "Come now. Papa can find employment . . . as can I."

Her mother dropped face-down on the bed then, her sniffles increasing to full-blown sobs. Violet patted her back.

"What shall we do?" Mama's muffled wail floated up from the counterpane,

"I'll send Josie to tell our driver to ready our carriage while we pack. Half the household is still abed. We'll slip away and be hours from here before anyone even notices."

Mama lifted a tear-stained face. "Without a farewell?"

"It's the easiest ... kindest thing to do." She could well imagine the platitudes, the apologies ... Will trying to explain why he couldn't go forward with their marriage. No, she would avoid that discomfort. Spare herself that. And him.

It was well past the midday meal before anyone realized the Howard females had vanished.

His mother stormed into his office, interrupting him, Dec, and Max as they discussed potential investments other than the ones he had already made. He'd learned from his father's mistakes. He would not rely solely on the land as his father and grandfather had done. The fortune he acquired from marrying Violet would be invested wisely. He would make certain their future was secured. He didn't want their children faced with the burden of debt and uncertainty.

Worry gleamed in his mother's eyes as she stopped before him. "She's gone!"

"Who is gone?"

"Miss Howard! Violet and her mother! They've left."

He rose slowly to his feet. "What do you mean? They're not in the house? Have you searched—"

"Oh, they are well and truly gone. They took their carriage and servants and left."

He strode past her, marching up the stairs and straight for Violet's bedchamber as though he could find evidence to the contrary of his mother's shocking words. He flung the door open to find the chamber empty, bed still unmade, doors to the armoire wide open, stripped bare inside.

He paced the room, feeling like a caged animal. He

stopped near the bed, dragging his hands through his hair and tugging hard. Where was she? Where had she gone? *And why?*

His mind tracked over their last conversation, trying to recall if she had given any indication that she was going to run. There had been tension, but she had seemed committed to the idea of their marriage. He had not suspected she would resort to running away.

Lowering his hands from his hair, he noticed a piece of parchment on the bed. He leaned down and plucked it from the rumpled covers, his eyes scanning the scrawl of handwriting, understanding at once why she left.

With a curse, he wadded the missive in his fist and flung it across the room.

They drove through the day, stopping only to refresh horses. Violet would have preferred they move at a faster pace, but with the accumulation of snow they could only travel so quickly. Not without risking themselves. As it were, they were weary when they finally stopped for the night at an inn.

The driver and groom saw to the horse as Violet, her mother, and the two maids slogged through the snow into the busy inn. It was Christmas Eve, she remembered dully as they stepped into the boisterous taproom.

It was some moments before their presence was even noted by the ruddy-faced innkeeper. He tore himself away from the small group of carolers near the fire.

"Ladies," he greeted in a booming voice. "Welcome, welcome! Happy Christmas!"

"Happy Christmas," she returned hollowly.

Her mother forced a wan smile. She had ceased to cry some hours ago, but Violet was well aware that her composure was only thinly-won. She could crumble again at the slightest provocation.

"We should like two rooms."

"One," Violet quickly corrected her mother. Their maids could share a room with them. Gone was the lifestyle they were accustomed to. If they could economize and return home with some of their funds, the better off they would be.

"Of course, come sit and warm yourselves by the fire and I'll have a room readied for you." He led them to a table, snapping for a serving girl to fetch some warmed wine.

Usually her mother refrained from spirits, but she eagerly accepted the drink, consumed it, and then held her goblet out for more.

"We have a lovely pheasant and potatoes prepared this evening if—"

"That sounds delicious." Violet nodded, caring little to hear the menu. She simply required food and a bed. Darkness where she could bury her face in a pillow and weep out her heartache in silent tears.

Will would know she was gone by now and he would know why. She had deliberately left the letter to be found. No other explanation was needed. He would understand. He was likely grateful she had taken her leave, sparing them both an uncomfortable scene.

Violet and her mother ate in brooding silence, watching the merriment unfolding around them, seeming to mock their dour mood.

"Would you ladies care for our mint pudding?"

Violet shook her head and then stopped at her mother's vigorous nod. "Yes, thank you."

Apparently she would not be escaping upstairs just yet. The innkeeper scurried off, skirting some dancing couples. The same couples passed their table, bumping it in their movements.

Violet winced, righting her empty cup where it had fallen. Would this wretched day ever end so she could lick her wounds in solitude?

Sudden cold whipped into the taproom as the heavy wood door opened and three tall figures stepped inside. Everything within her froze. Her lungs seized, air ceasing to flow. The three men stood there, filling the threshold. Even bundled in greatcoats, she recognized them. Her gaze sharpened on the man in the center. Merlton. *Will.*

Her mother noticed the earl and his friends, as well, squeaking her alarm and dropping her spoon with a clatter. "Violet! What . . . how? I told you we should have explained and made our farewells—"

Violet covered her mother's hand with one of her own, silencing her. Will scanned the room, and in those few moments she debated fleeing, hiding somewhere in the inn. Until he spotted her and put an end to such frantic thoughts.

His gaze narrowed on her. His purposeful strides carried him across the room toward her. She rose to her feet, lifting her chin. "Lord Merlton—"

His eyes flashed as he closed the distance between them and latched onto her wrist, pulling her around the table. "I told you to call me Will."

She dug in her heels, resisting him. "Stop! You don't understand. I left the letter for you to—"

He stopped and shoved his face close to hers. "I saw your bloody letter!"

"Then you understand—"

"I understand a good deal more than you do if you think you can just skulk away without a by-your-leave!"

Her eyes widened at his fierce expression. He was correct. She didn't understand. She didn't understand at all. Why he was here?

She moistened her lips. "In lieu of my change in circumstances, I thought you would appreciate my discretion—"

"Appreciate? I made a promise to you—"

"Is that what this is about? I've injured your pride? Have no fear, I release you from your promise."

"Anything amiss here?" A voice intruded. "This man bothering you, Miss?"

Violet's gaze flicked to a man that rose from a nearby table. He looked like a farmer, brawny and thick-fisted. He sat with several other men of similar appearance dressed in modest wool.

Will didn't even glance their way. His gaze remained fixed on her, his expression almost desperate in its intensity.

She inhaled a deep breath. Apparently that uncomfortable conversation she had hoped to avoid would have to happen, after all. In front of a roomful of strangers, no less.

"I'm sorry, Will. I can't give you what you want . . . what you need. I'm not an heiress anymore."

He gripped her arms and gave her a small shake, his eyes deep and penetrating, reaching that part of her that wanted to curl into a small ball in the dark and weep until all tears were spent. "Can't you see—"

"All right there, that's enough now." Suddenly the farmer grabbed Will and wrenched him from Violet. With an inhuman cry, Will swung at the man, his fist connecting in a sickening crunch of bone on bone.

Violet grabbed her mother's hand, lifted her skirts and ran for the stairs, dragging her mother after her just as the room erupted into chaos.

"Violet!"

At the roar of her name, she glanced behind her and felt her eyes widen at the sight of Will being held back by several men. The duke and viscount had entered the fray and were likewise engaged, swinging fists and attempting to pull men off Will. One farmer punched Will in the side of the face and he went down.

Violet cried out, her heart lurching to her throat. She released her mother and staggered forward. "Stop! Will, just stop!" Tears rose up in her throat, garbling her words. "You don't have to do this. I can't marry you! You're free to—"

Will surged back to his feet, indifferent to his bloodied lip. He was crazed and still fighting despite the men striking him and the innkeeper shouting for him to leave.

"Please!" Violet called. "Don't hurt him!"

He roared her name over the din. "Violet! I don't give a bloody damn about the money!"

Her mother was there then, clasping her arm urgently in clenching fingers. "Did you hear him, Vi? Did you hear him?"

She shook her head in disbelief, her heart pounding so hard it hurt in her chest.

"Will," she whispered.

"Violet!" her mother choked, but Violet didn't look at her. She couldn't. She could only stare at Will . . . could only see his face, find his eyes amid the melee.

"Violet! I love you, Violet!"

A sob broke from her lips and she rushed forward, shoving through the press of bodies, stumbling over broken dishes and crushed holly.

She struck one of the farmers with her fist, her hand bouncing ineffectually off his massive shoulder. "Unhand him! Unhand him, I tell you."

"Gor! What the—"

She glared at him. "Unhand him, you brute! That's my fiancé!"

He relinquished his hold on Will enough for her to wedge between the others and wrap her arms around him.

Will swept her up against him with one arm. "Violet, I'm a bloody fool. I should have told you before. . . ."

She shook her head. "I can't fault you for not saying what I didn't have the courage to confess as well. I love you, Will."

His hand cupped her face, his fingers caressing her cheek almost reverently.

Her heart sank as she suddenly recalled that he still needed an heiress, and she was no longer that. "But my father lost everything, Will. I haven't anything. I can bring you nothing."

He hushed her with his fingers on her lips. "I don't care. I will figure it out. You mustn't worry. I have hopes for some investments I've made, but even if they shouldn't produce results, we'll be fine. As long as we're together. We'll make it work. Violet, the reason I haven't wed an heiress in all these years is because I could love none of them. You were the first to move me, the first and only I've loved. You . . . you bring me everything."

Her heart swelled then, emotion clogging her throat. His mouth claimed hers. Dimly, she registered clapping and cheers, but she acknowledged none of it.

She didn't look up. There was only this. Will's lips on hers. Will's arms wrapped around her. There was only love.

Keep reading for an excerpt from
New York Times bestselling author Sophie Jordan's
first book in The Debutante Files:

A GOOD DEBUTANTE'S GUIDE TO RUIN

Available now wherever books are sold.

The last woman on earth he would ever touch . . .

Declan, the Duke of Banbury, has no interest in ushering Rosalie Hughes, his stepsister, into society. Dumped on him with nowhere else to go, he's determined to rid himself of the headstrong debutante by bestowing on her an obscenely large dowry . . . making her the most sought-after heiress of the Season.

. . . is about to become the only one he wants

But Rosalie isn't about to go along with Declan's plans. Surrounded by fortune hunters, how is she supposed to find a man who truly wants her? Taking control of her fate, Rosalie dons a disguise and sneaks into Sodom, a private club host to all manner of illicit activity—and frequented by her infuriatingly handsome stepbrother.

In a shadowed alcove, Declan can't resist the masked temptress who sets his blood afire . . . any more than Rosalie can deny her longing for a man who will send her into ruin.

An Excerpt from

A GOOD DEBUTANTE'S GUIDE TO RUIN

Rain hung thick in the air, the threat of which turned the early evening gray and mist-shrouded. Mrs. Heathstone knocked smartly on the immense double doors of the Duke of Banbury's Mayfair residence.

Rosalie slid an anxious glance down her body and winced, smoothing a hand over the well-worn wool of her cloak. *Serviceable.* That's the word that came to mind. *Shabby.* That was another word.

It wasn't how Rosalie envisioned her return to London. She dreamt of bright skies and heralding trumpets. Ridiculous, but what fantasy didn't possess a touch of the absurd? At least for her. She was an expert at dreaming up the absurd. She had imagined returning a debutante of the first order, outfitted in a wardrobe that royalty would envy. With swains lining up to pay court on her. With parties and galas that kept her out all hours. An invitation to court from the queen herself. She had imagined all this and more.

She had imagined him.

The words whispered through her mind and made her wince. Perhaps not precisely *him*. Only someone as handsome as her stepbrother. Whenever she imagined a suitor for herself, he always bore a striking resemblance to Declan. She supposed it was a testament to her lack of exposure to suitable gentlemen during her time at the Harwich School for Young Ladies. Certainly some time about Town would dash such day dreams.

She sighed. Daydreams had long kept her company as she rusticated in Yorkshire, waiting for her mother to claim her. Waiting for a Season. Waiting for her life to begin. She had perfected waiting to an art form.

Now, standing on Declan's stoop, the cold evening vapor folding over her, those fantasies were a very distant thing. But at least the wait was finally over. She stood two steps below Mrs. Heathstone's formidable personage. The headmistress was taller than any man of Rosalie's limited acquaintance even without the advantage of said steps.

She huddled deeper into her cloak as Mrs. Heathstone rapped yet again. The sound reverberated out onto the street, and Rosalie shifted nervously on her feet, casting uneasy glances over her shoulder, certain that eyes were already upon them from every neighboring window, wondering at the bedraggled pair calling upon the Duke of Banbury.

The mist suddenly gave way to rain as though it could be denied no longer.

"Drat!" Mrs. Heathstone growled, throwing a gloved hand over her head as if that would offer some protection.

Rosalie shrank back inside the voluminous hood of her

cloak. She knew from experience that the slightest moisture turned her hair into a wild, frizzy mess. She pushed a coppery curl behind her ear. There was no help for it. She would not be making a sterling impression this eve. Of course, until this moment she had not realized how very important it was to her that she do so. She had told herself through the entire journey here that he would likely not even remember her.

"Perhaps we should call again later?" The ring of hope in her suggestion was unmistakable even over the drum of rain.

"Nonsense. Someone is at home."

Of course, *someone* was at home. The duke maintained a staff of dozens at his Town residence, but the gentleman himself? The gentleman they needed to see? He was unlikely to be home. A matter of circumstance that appeared to only bear consequence to Rosalie. Mrs. Heathstone was quite prepared to deposit her on the duke's threshold and then bolt. The headmistress had made up her mind weeks ago when she arranged this trip, and she was not to be dissuaded. As she had regretfully explained again and again, the duke was family. If her mother would not step up to claim her, then responsibility fell to him.

At last the door opened.

It was the only invitation Mrs. Heathstone required. She charged inside, shoving past a sputtering butler. Rosalie ascended, hesitating on the top step, peering inside the grand foyer that was at once familiar and alien. She knew it shouldn't look so large and formidable now that she was a woman grown and no longer a child, but it actually looked bigger.

Mrs. Heathstone shook her cloak, spraying water onto the marble floor as she flung back her hood, revealing her lush silvery gray hair. Her sharp eyes narrowed on Rosalie. "Miss Hughes, come inside at once before you catch ague." Her long, elegant fingers flicked impatiently on the air.

Rosalie obediently stepped inside, looking in awe up at the high-domed frescoed ceiling. Lowering her gaze, she sent the butler a small smile. She did not recognize him, but then she wouldn't. She had been very young the last time she visited here. She had been relegated to the duke's country estate most of the time. Her mother preferred it that way. Preferred to have her in the country while she entertained in Town. Out of sight. Out of mind.

The butler's face puffed like a bloated fish. "Madame, you cannot barge in here—"

"Oh, no worry, I'm not staying." She dropped Rosalie's valise to the floor, her manner brisk and efficient as she closed her hands around Rosalie's shoulders. "Remember all you've been taught. You're a lady, Miss Hughes, no matter . . ." Her voice faded, but Rosalie knew what she was going to say.

No matter who or what your mother was.

"Yes, ma'am." She nodded.

Mrs. Heathstone squeezed her shoulders gently a final time. "You're a good girl, Rosalie. Smart, too. I wish we could have kept you on, but your future was never at Harwich's. Your future is in this world." She glanced around the opulent foyer.

Rosalie swallowed back her protest. This didn't feel like her world at all. For the last ten years she had shared a drafty room with Rachel, a former pupil like herself who now taught French at the school. Rachel had been top in their class and spoke French like she was born to it. When Mademoiselle

Leflore decided to return home to tend to an ailing aunt, Rachel had been offered the position.

Unfortunately, there was no position to be had for Rosalie. She had remained the last two years merely due to the goodwill of Mrs. Heathstone. She'd tried to make herself useful in that time. However, her situation was always awkward. Not a pupil and not an instructor. She merely took up space.

And yet her meager room back at Harwich felt more familiar——more like home——than these lavish surroundings.

She wasn't certain the Duke of Banbury would welcome her any more than her mother would, but Mrs. Heathstone was confidant this was the right course of action, and Rosalie acknowledged that something had to change. She could not live on the charity of others. She should have left two years ago.

"Thank you, Mrs. Heathstone." She nodded jerkily, emotion clogging her throat. In many ways, this woman was the closest thing she ever had to a mother. "For everything."

Smiling, the headmistress brushed her cheek with gloved fingertips. "Dear girl. Take care of yourself."

And then she was gone. Rosalie watched as she swept out the door, her chest tight and achy. She rubbed gloved fingers against her breastbone, willing herself to be brave. To embrace this next phase of her life.

The butler sputtered anew, and Rosalie sent him a half-hearted smile as she smoothed her hands down the front of her damp cloak.

"Good evening," she greeted him, her voice a fraction too squeaky.

"You cannot be here." The butler looked her up and down with the faintest curl of his lip. "His Grace is not at home at the moment to receive—"

"I shall wait for him." She lifted her chin, attempting to emulate Mrs. Heathstone's haughtiness.

"That is not possible, Miss . . ."

"Hughes," she supplied. "Rosalie Hughes." At the butler's blank stare, she elaborated. "The duke's stepsister."

Her announcement was met with a moment of stunned silence. Deciding not to give him too long to consider this revelation——and why the duke's stepsister had been relatively absent for the last seven years——she brushed past him and moved toward what she hoped was the drawing room. Her memory could not recall.

She walked up the stairs, her gloved hand skimming the ornate stone balustrade as though she knew where she was going. "I'll wait in the drawing room," she called over her shoulder as she reached the second floor. Hoping she chose the correct room, she pushed open the double doors to the first room on her right. She breathed in relief. Her guess was accurate.

The butler followed her inside, hovering close but saying nothing even though he looked mightily tempted. It was a masculine room, full of rich colors and dark wood furniture. A fire crackled in the massive hearth, drawing her forward, her boots sinking deep into the plush Aubusson rug. Rosalie sank down on a blue oversized settee on the far side of the room that was angled toward the fireplace. She dropped her valise at her feet and held out her hands, greedy for the warmth.

She stared solemnly at the butler, hoping to convey an air of . . . belonging. "I'll wait His Grace's audience in here." Somehow, miraculously, her words rang with confidence.

His shoulders slumped slightly and she knew, in that moment, he had capitulated.

"Very well. Can I fetch you any refreshments as you wait, Miss Hughes?"

Her stomach rumbled at the offer. She had not eaten since their last stop several hours ago. "Yes, that would be lovely." She was grateful her voice did not quiver with her eagerness.

With a nod, he departed, slow to take his gaze off her, slow to turn and present her with his very ramrod back. As though he could not quite reconcile a female of her humble appearance in the duke's vaunted drawing room. She could understand that. She could scarcely reconcile it herself.

As soon as the door clicked behind him, she relaxed and fell back on the settee. It felt as though she had just succeeded in some grand deception.

She winced and tried to remind herself that she had every right to call on the Duke of Banbury. Especially considering the unavailability of her own mother. What else was she to do? She was a gentlewoman. A lady. She nodded to herself as Mrs. Heathstone's arguments played silently in her mind.

Her stepbrother would not turn her away. True, he had not responded to Mrs. Heathstone's letter, but Mrs. Heathstone insisted he would do his duty. Rosalie hoped she was correct.

She bit into her bottom lip, gnawing it until she forced herself to stop. She didn't need a bloodied lip when she came face-to-face with Declan. She blinked hard and long, reprimanding herself. He was no longer Declan to her. She must not think of him so informally. He was a duke now and as far removed from her as the moon. A man full grown. She must forget the boy she remembered with such fondness. Oh, very well. With such adoration. Natural, she supposed. So often relegated to the country together, he had accepted her. Five years her senior, he had not minded when she traipsed after him. He even rescued her from a tree a time or two. She was always climbing trees. And always managing to get herself stuck. *Come, Carrots,* he would beckon her with waving hands and wide, encouraging eyes. *Come down. I'll catch you.*

A maid entered the room pushing a cart. She smiled at Rosalie shyly and bobbed a tiny curtsy.

"Thank you. I'll serve myself."

"Yes, miss."

With another bob of her head, she left Rosalie alone.

She fell upon the tray, making short work of the tea and delicious frosted cakes and tiny sandwiches. She ate everything and then regretted it, eyeing the crumbs. She would appear a graceless sloth when they come to claim the cart.

She collapsed back on the settee, with little refinement one hand rubbing her full belly, the other idly stroking the elegant brocade pillow beside her. She blew out a repleted sigh and glanced around the well-appointed room. An enormous painting depicting Persephone's abduction hung along a wall, taking nearly the entire space. It was riveting. Bold and dramatic. The dark Hades clasped the fair Persephone about the waist, one large hand splayed just below the swell of a breast that threatened to spill from her white tunic as he pulled her into the murky cavern of hell lined with demons and skeletons. Rosalie swallowed, her stare fixing on Hades' feral expression, clearly intent on possession. Something curled in her belly at the idea of a man *wanting, needing* a woman that much.

The clock on the mantel ticked in the silence of the room. Only the occasional pop from the fire interrupted the still. She yawned widely into her hand. The journey had taken its toll. She had not left Harwich in ten years. No visits anywhere. She was unaccustomed to the rigors of travel.

Her head lolled against the back of the sofa, grateful that she was turned partially from the door, not in full sight of anyone upon first entering the room. She'd hear them before they spotted her. It would give her time to compose herself.

The warmth of the fire licked over her and her limbs grew boneless. This was the most comfortable she had felt since leaving Yorkshire.

Her eyes drifted shut. Just for a moment she would rest them. She snuggled drowsily into the sofa. No doubt the duke would arrive soon. She'd hear his approach. Better yet, she'd hear the approach of the maid when she returned to reclaim the cart.

For just a moment she would rest her eyes.

ABOUT THE AUTHOR

SOPHIE JORDAN grew up in the Texas hill country where she wove fantasies of dragons, warriors, and princesses. A former high school English teacher, she's the *New York Times*, *USA Today*, and international bestselling author of more than twenty novels. She now lives in Houston with her family. When she's not writing, she spends her time overloading on caffeine (lattes preferred), talking plotlines with anyone who will listen (including her kids), and cramming her DVR with anything that has a happily ever after. You can visit her online at www.sophiejordan.net.

Discover great authors, exclusive offers, and more at hc.com.

Give in to your impulses . . .
Read on for a sneak peek at five brand-new
e-book original tales of romance
from Avon Impulse.
Available now wherever e-books are sold.

VARIOUS STATES OF UNDRESS: VIRGINIA
By Laura Simcox

THE GOVERNESS CLUB: LOUISA
By Ellie Macdonald

GOOD GUYS WEAR BLACK
By Lizbeth Selvig

SINFUL REWARDS 1
A BILLIONAIRES AND BIKERS NOVELLA
By Cynthia Sax

COVERING KENDALL
A LOVE AND FOOTBALL NOVEL
By Julie Brannagh

An Excerpt from

VARIOUS STATES OF UNDRESS: VIRGINIA

by Laura Simcox

If she had it her way, Virginia Fulton—daughter of
the President of the United States—would spend
more time dancing in Manhattan's nightclubs than
working in its skyscrapers. But when she finds
herself in the arms of sexy, persuasive Dexter
Cameron, who presents her with the opportunity
of a lifetime, Virginia sees it as a sign . . . but
can she take it without losing her heart?

Virginia threw her hands in the air and walked over to face him. "Come on, Dex! Be realistic. You need a *team* to fix this store. An army."

"So hire one." He leaned toward her. "I need you. And you need me."

"I don't need you." She narrowed her eyes. There was no way she was going to tell him about dumping Owlton. Not right now, anyway.

Dex slid off the desk and covered the few feet between them, frowning. "Yes, you do," he said.

She stared at his mouth, her legs suddenly feeling wobbly. "No, I don't." She raised her hands to his shoulders to steady herself.

"You can choose to keep telling yourself that, or you can make a move."

"What do you mean by that?"

"Move forward."

She took a deep breath. "I don't know if I can." The words came out raspy, and the look of irritation in Dex's eyes changed into something much more focused. He hesitated for a moment and then leaned closer. "Make a leap of faith, trust your instincts, and take the job. You'll have my full support."

As she gazed up into his steady eyes, she was all too aware of her fear. Because of cowardice, she never acted as if she expected anyone to take her seriously—and so they didn't. It pissed her off. She didn't like being pissed, especially not at herself. Dex took her seriously, didn't he? She closed her eyes. "Okay. I'll do it."

When she opened them, he smiled. "Great. Now ... about moving forward?"

"Yeah?"

"*Literally* moving forward would be fantastic. I never got to kiss you back, you know."

"I ... didn't expect you to," she said.

"That might be, but the more I thought about your kiss last night, the more necessary kissing you back became to me. And now? I can't think about much else."

She gripped his shoulders and gazed into his eyes. "To be honest, neither can I."

"Please tell me we can try again. Kiss me and see what happens." His voice was low and thick.

Virginia's legs almost gave out from under her, and a shuddering breath left her body. She should be taking a step back, not contemplating kissing him again. Her body swayed forward, and she tightened her grip on his shoulders to steady herself. Just as she closed her eyes to think, his mouth descended, hot and sweet, angling over hers and stopping a hairsbreadth from her lips.

"Mmm," he uttered, the sound coming from deep in his throat, and it was all she needed.

She pushed up onto her toes, her fingers laced behind his neck, and she kissed him. He tasted earthy—wild, almost—

and that surprising discovery sent a shock wave through her brain. She kissed him again. "More," she murmured, even though she knew she shouldn't. His tongue invaded her mouth; he turned and, in one motion, lifted her onto the desk. Electricity sang through her body, and, as she twined her tongue with his, the idea of *shouldn't* started to become hazy. Her hands threaded through his cropped hair and she leaned back—arching her breasts toward him—wanting Dex to press her down with his body. *Please*, she whispered in her mind, *Please, Dex.*

His hands ran over her hips, but he didn't move closer, so she deepened the kiss, letting her hands trail over his smooth jaw, the taut sides of his neck; then she slid her fingers around the lapels of his suit and tugged. With a groan, Dex pulled her against his chest again, his hands skimming up her back to gently tug on the blunt ends of her hair. She complied, letting her head fall back, and his hot, open mouth slid down her throat and nestled in the crook of her neck. He kissed her there, lingering.

"More," she gasped out loud, clinging to his shoulders.

He kissed her throat again, his tongue branding a circle under her jaw. Then slowly, he pulled away. "We have to stop," he said, looking into her eyes. "If we don't . . ." He swallowed and she watched his throat work. She hadn't gotten to kiss him there, yet. Dipping her chin, she leaned forward, but he pulled away. He gave her a sheepish smile. "I think we sealed the deal, don't you?

An Excerpt from

THE GOVERNESS CLUB: LOUISA

by Ellie Macdonald

Louisa Brockhurst is on the run—from her friends, from her family, even from her dream of independence through the Governess Club. Handsome but menacing John Taylor is a prizefighter-turned-innkeeper who is trying to make his way in society. When Louisa shows up at his doorstep, he's quick to accept her offer to help—at a price. Their attraction grows, but will headstrong, fiery Louisa ever trust the surprisingly kind John enough to tell him the dangerous secrets from her past that keep her running?

Her eyes followed his movements as he straightened. Good Lord, but the moniker "Giant Johnny" was highly appropriate. The man was a mountain. A fleeting thought crossed her mind about what it would be like to have those large arms encompass her.

He spied her packed portmanteau and looked at her questioningly. "You are moving on? I thought your plans were unconfirmed."

Louisa lifted her chin. "They are. But that does not mean I must stay here in order to solidify them."

He put his thick hands on his hips, doubling his width. "But it also means that you do not have to leave in order to do so." She opened her mouth to speak, but he stayed her with his hand. "I understand what it is like to be adrift. If you wish, you can remain here. It is clear that I need help, a woman's help." He gestured to the room. "I have little notion and less inclination for cleaning. I need someone to take charge in this area. Will you do it?"

Louisa stared at him. *Help him by being a maid? In an inn?* Of all the things she had considered doing, working in such a place had never crossed her mind. She was not suited for such work. A governess, a companion, yes—but a maid?

What would her mother have said about this? Or any of her family?

She pressed her lips together. It had been six years since she'd allowed her family to influence her, and this job would at least keep her protected from the elements. She would be able to protect herself from the more unruly patrons, she was certain. It would be hard-earned coin, to be sure, but the current condition of her moneybag would not object to whichever manner she earned more. It would indeed present the biggest challenge she had yet faced, but how hard could it be?

"What say you, Mrs. Brock?"

His voice drew her out of her thoughts. Regarding him carefully, Louisa knew better than just to accept his offer. "What sorts of benefits could I expect?"

"Proper wage, meals, and a room." His answer was quick.

"How many meals?"

"How many does the average person eat?" he countered. "Three by my count."

Would her stomach survive three meals of such fare? She nodded. "This room? Or a smaller one in the attic?" She had slept in her fair share of small rooms as a governess; she would fight for the biggest one she could get.

"This one is fine. This is not a busy inn, so it can be spared." He rubbed his bald head. "My room is behind the office, so you will never be alone on the premises."

Hm. "I see. Free days?" Not that she expected to need them. She knew no one in the area and had no plans to inform her friends—her *former* friends—of where she was.

"Once a fortnight."

"And my duties?"

"Cleaning, of course. Helping out in the kitchen and pub when necessary."

"Was last night a typical crowd?" she asked.

"Yes. Local men come here regularly. There are not many places a man in this area can go."

"And the women? I am curious."

He shrugged his boulder shoulders. "None have yet come in here. I don't cater to their tastes."

Louisa sniffed and glanced around the room. The condition truly was atrocious. If the other rooms were like this, it would take days of hard work to get them up to scratch. It would be an accomplishment to be proud of, if she succeeded.

Ha—if I succeed? I always succeed.

She looked back at Giant Johnny, watching her with his hands on his hips, legs braced apart. She eyed him. He stood like a sportsman, sure of his ground and his strength. A sliver of awareness slipped through her at the confidence he exuded. This man was capable of many things; she was certain of it.

And if she were to agree to his offer, she would be with him every day. This mountain, this behemoth, would have authority over her as her employer. It was not the proximity to the giant that worried her; it was that last fact.

It rankled. For so long she had wished for independence, had almost achieved it with her friends and the formation of the Governess Club, only to have it collapse underneath her. And now she found herself once again having to submit to a man's authority.

It was a bitter pill to swallow. She would have to trust that she would eventually be able to turn the situation to her advantage. Nodding, she said, "I accept the position, Mr. Taylor."

An Excerpt from

GOOD GUYS WEAR BLACK

by Lizbeth Selvig

When single mom Rose Hanrahan arrives in
Kennison Falls, Minnesota, as the new head
librarian, she instantly clashes with hometown
hero Dewey Mitchell over just about everything.
But in a small town like Kennison Falls,
it's tough to ignore anybody, and the more
they're thrown together, the more it seems
like fate has something in store for them.

Waves of anger, like blasts of heat, rolled off the woman as she turned to the pumps. Rooted to the spot, Dewey watched the scene, studying the mystifying child. He was standing a little too close to the gas fumes, but irritation took a reluctant backseat to curiosity and captivation. What kind of kid couldn't follow a simple directive from people in uniform? What nine- or ten-year-old kid knew the year, make, and model of a fourteen-year-old fire truck, not to mention its specs—right down to the capacities of its foam firefighting equipment?

Asperger's syndrome. He knew the phrase but little about it. He certainly believed there were real syndromes out there, since he'd seen plenty of strange behavior in his life. But this reeked of a pissed-off mother simply warning him away from her weird kid. He knew in this day and age you weren't supposed to touch a child, but, damn it, the kid could have gotten seriously hurt. And she sure as hell hadn't been around.

Then there was the car. Over ten years old and spotless as new. The red GT did *not* fit the woman. Or the situation. You just didn't expect to see a mom and her son driving cross-country in a fireball-red sports car. She had some sort of mild, uppity accent and used words like "ire." In a way, she wasn't any more normal than her kid.

He tried to turn away. She wasn't from town, so he wouldn't have to think about her once the gas was pumped. But something compelled him to watch her finish—something that told him the world would go back to being a lot less interesting once she'd left it.

She let the boy hang the nozzle up, and then did something amazing. She opened her door, took out what appeared to be a chamois, and bent over the gas tank door to wipe and buff an area where gas must have dripped.

She doesn't deserve it if she doesn't know how to take care of it. That's what he'd said about her.

Dang. She sure knew how to keep it . . . red.

His observations were cut off by a sudden wail. The boy lunged like a spaniel after a squirrel. The woman grabbed him, squatted, and took his hands in hers, pressing his palms together like he was praying. Her mouth moved quickly, and she leaned in close, her forehead nearly but not quite touching her son's.

It should not have been a remotely sexy picture, but it was nearly as attractive as the sight of her polishing the Mustang. The over-reactive Mama Wolverine morphed into someone intense and sincere with desperation around the edges, and something he didn't understand at all tugged at him, deep in his gut.

The boy finally nodded and quit fussing. The woman dropped her hands and leaned forward to kiss him on the cheek. After straightening, she glanced over her shoulder, and the boy's wistful gaze followed. Dewey remembered that he'd begged only to look at the gauges on the truck. Should he just give in and let the kid have his look?

Then everything soft about the mother hardened as she met Dewey's eyes. Her delicately angled features tightened like sharp weapons, and the wisps of hair escaping from a long, thick brown ponytail seemed to freeze in place as if they didn't dare move for fear of pissing her off further. She stood, her shapely legs—their calves bare and browned beneath the hems of knee-length cargo shorts—spread like a superhero's in front of her son. She didn't say a word, so neither did Dewey. He didn't need to take her on again. Let the kid look up the gauges online.

With a parting shot from her angry eyes, she ushered the boy into the passenger seat, darted to her side, and climbed in. The engine came to life and purred like a jungle cat. She clearly cared for the car the way she did for her son. Or somebody did.

However angry she was, she didn't take it out on the car but pulled smoothly away from the pump. Dewey smiled. It was her car all right. Had it not been, she'd have peeled out just to punctuate her feelings for him.

Impressive woman. A little crazy. But impressive.

An Excerpt from

SINFUL REWARDS 1
A Billionaires and Bikers Novella
by Cynthia Sax

Belinda "Bee" Carter is a good girl; at least, that's
what she tells herself. And a good girl deserves
a nice guy—just like the gorgeous and moody
billionaire Nicolas Rainer. Or so she thinks,
until she takes a look through her telescope
and sees a naked, tattooed man on the balcony
across the courtyard. He has been watching
her, and that makes him all the more enticing.
But when a mysterious and anonymous text
message dares her to do something bad, she
must decide if she is really the good girl she has
always claimed to be, or if she's willing to risk
everything for her secret fantasy of being watched.

An Avon Red Novella

I'd told Cyndi I'd never use it, that it was an instrument purchased by perverts to spy on their neighbors. She'd laughed and called me a prude, not knowing that I was one of those perverts, that I secretly yearned to watch and be watched, to care and be cared for.

If I'm cautious, and I'm always cautious, she'll never realize I used her telescope this morning. I swing the tube toward the bench and adjust the knob, bringing the mysterious object into focus.

It's a phone. Nicolas's phone. I bounce on the balls of my feet. This is a sign, another declaration from fate that we belong together. I'll return Nicolas's much-needed device to him. As a thank you, he'll invite me to dinner. We'll talk. He'll realize how perfect I am for him, fall in love with me, marry me.

Cyndi will find a fiancé also—everyone loves her—and we'll have a double wedding, as sisters of the heart often do. It'll be the first wedding my family has had in generations.

Everyone will watch us as we walk down the aisle. I'll wear a strapless white Vera Wang mermaid gown with organza and lace details, crystal and pearl embroidery accents, the bodice fitted, and the skirt hemmed for my shorter height. My hair will be swept up. My shoes—

Voices murmur outside the condo's door, the sound piercing my delightful daydream. I swing the telescope upward, not wanting to be caught using it. The snippets of conversation drift away.

I don't relax. If the telescope isn't positioned in the same way as it was last night, Cyndi will realize I've been using it. She'll tease me about being a fellow pervert, sharing the story, embellished for dramatic effect, with her stern, serious dad—or, worse, with Angel, that snobby friend of hers.

I'll die. It'll be worse than being the butt of jokes in high school because that ridicule was about my clothes and this will center on the part of my soul I've always kept hidden. It'll also be the truth, and I won't be able to deny it. I am a pervert.

I have to return the telescope to its original position. This is the only acceptable solution. I tap the metal tube.

Last night, my man-crazy roommate was giggling over the new guy in three-eleven north. The previous occupant was a gray-haired, bowtie-wearing tax auditor, his luxurious accommodations supplied by Nicolas. The most exciting thing he ever did was drink his tea on the balcony.

According to Cyndi, the new occupant is a delicious piece of man candy—tattooed, buff, and head-to-toe lickable. He was completing armcurls outside, and she enthusiastically counted his reps, oohing and aahing over his bulging biceps, calling to me to take a look.

I resisted that temptation, focusing on making macaroni and cheese for the two of us, the recipe snagged from the diner my mom works in. After we scarfed down dinner, Cyndi licking her plate clean, she left for the club and hasn't returned.

Three-eleven north is the mirror condo to ours. I

straighten the telescope. That position looks about right, but then, the imitation UGGs I bought in my second year of college looked about right also. The first time I wore the boots in the rain, the sheepskin fell apart, leaving me barefoot in Economics 201.

Unwilling to risk Cyndi's friendship on "about right," I gaze through the eyepiece. The view consists of rippling golden planes, almost like . . .

Tanned skin pulled over defined abs.

I blink. It can't be. I take another look. A perfect pearl of perspiration clings to a puckered scar. The drop elongates more and more, stretching, snapping. It trickles downward, navigating the swells and valleys of a man's honed torso.

No. I straighten. This is wrong. I shouldn't watch our sexy neighbor as he stands on his balcony. If anyone catches me . . .

Parts 1, 2, 3, and 4 available now!

An Excerpt from

COVERING KENDALL
A Love and Football Novel

by Julie Brannagh

Kendall Tracy, General Manager of the San
Francisco Miners, is not one for rash decisions
or one-night stands. But when she finds herself
alone in a hotel room with a heart-stoppingly
gorgeous man—who looks oddly familiar—
Kendall throws her own rules out the window . . .

Drew McCoy *should* look familiar; he's a star player
for her team's archrival, the Seattle Sharks.
They agree to pretend their encounter never
happened. But staying away from each
other is harder than it seems, and they both
discover that some risks are worth taking.

"You're Drew McCoy," she cried out.

She scooted to the edge of the bed, clutching the sheet around her torso as she went. It was a little late now for modesty. Retaining some shred of dignity might be a good thing.

She'd watched Drew's game film with the coaching staff. She'd seen his commercials for hair products and sports drinks and soup a hundred times before. His contract with the Sharks was done as of the end of football season, and the Miners wanted him to play for them. Drew was San Francisco's number-one target in next season's free agency. She'd planned on asking the team's owner to write a big check to Drew and his agent next March. And if all that wasn't enough, Drew was eight years younger than she was.

What the hell was wrong with her? It must have been the knit hat covering his famous hair, or finding him in a non-jock hangout like a bookstore. Maybe it was the temporary insanity brought on by an overwhelming surge of hormones.

"Is there a problem?" he said.

"I can't have anything to do with you. I have to go."

He shook his head in adorable confusion. She couldn't think of anything she wanted more right now than to run her fingers through his gorgeous hair.

"This is your hotel room. Where do you think you're going?"

She yanked as much of the sheet off the bed as possible, attempting to wrap it around herself and stand up at the same time. He was simultaneously grabbing at the comforter to shield himself. It didn't work.

She twisted her foot in the bedding while she hurled herself away from him and ended up on the carpet seconds later in a tangle of sheets and limbs, still naked. Her butt hit the floor so hard she almost expected to bounce.

The number-one reason Kendall didn't engage in one-night stands as a habit hauled himself up on all fours in the middle of the bed. Out of all the guys in the world available for a short-term fling, of *course* she'd pick the man who could get her fired or sued.

He grabbed the robe he'd slung over the foot of the bed, scrambled off the mattress, and jammed his arms into the sleeves as he advanced on her.

"Are you okay? You went down pretty hard." His eyes skimmed over her. "That's going to leave a mark."

He crouched next to her as he reached out to help her up. She resisted the impulse to stare at golden skin, an eight-pack, and a sizable erection. She'd heard Drew didn't lack for dates. He had things to offer besides the balance in his bank accounts.

"I'm okay," she told him.

She felt a little shaky. She'd probably have a nice bruise later. She was going down all right, and it had nothing to do with sex. It had everything to do with the fact that, if anyone from the Miners organization saw him emerging from her room in the next seventy-two hours, she was in the kind of trouble with her employer there was no recovering from. The interim general manager of an NFL team did not sleep with anyone from the opposing team, especially when the two teams were archrivals that hated each other with the heat of a thousand suns. Especially when the guy was a star player her own organization was more than a little interested in acquiring. *Especially* before a game that could mean the inside track to the playoffs for both teams.

Drew and Kendall would be the Romeo and Juliet of the NFL. Well, without all the dying. Death by 24/7 sports media embarrassment didn't count.

He reached out, grabbed her beneath the armpits, and hoisted her off the floor like she weighed nothing.

"I've got you. Let's see if you can stand up," he said. His warm, gentle hands moved over her, looking for injuries. "Why don't you lean on me for a second here?"

She tried rewrapping the sheet around her so she could walk away from him while preserving her dignity. It wasn't going to happen. She couldn't stop staring at him. If she let him take her in his arms, she'd be lost. She teetered as she leaned against the hotel room wall.

"I'm—I'm fine. I—"

"Hold still," he said. She heard his bare feet slap against the carpeting as he grabbed the second robe out of the coat closet and brought it back to her. "If you don't want to do this, that's your decision, but I don't understand what's wrong."

She struggled into the thick terry robe as she tried to think of a response. He was staring at her as she retrieved the belt and swathed herself in yards of fabric. Judging by his continuing erection, he liked what he saw, even if it was covered up from her neck to below her knees. He licked his bottom lip. Her mouth went dry. Damn it.

Of *course* the most attractive guy she'd been anywhere near a bed with in the past year was completely off-limits.

"You don't recognize me," she said.

"No, I don't," he said. "Is there a problem?"

"You might say that." She finally succeeded in knotting the belt of the robe around her waist, dropped the sheet at her feet, and stuck out one hand. "Hi. I'm Kendall Tracy. I'm the interim GM of the San Francisco Miners." His eyes widened in shock. "Nice to meet you."